the RIGHT RANGER

THE MEN OF
AT EASE RANCH

the RIGHT RanGeR

THE MEN OF
AT EASE RANCH

DONNA MICHAELS

This book is a work of fiction. Names, characters, places, and incidents are the product of the author's imagination or are used fictitiously. Any resemblance to actual events, locales, or persons, living or dead, is coincidental.

Copyright © 2017 by Donna Michaels. All rights reserved, including the right to reproduce, distribute, or transmit in any form or by any means. For information regarding subsidiary rights, please contact the Publisher.

Entangled Publishing, LLC
2614 South Timberline Road
Suite 109
Fort Collins, CO 80525
Visit our website at www.entangledpublishing.com.

Lovestruck is an imprint of Entangled Publishing, LLC.

Edited by Heather Howland
Cover design by Heather Howland
Cover art from iStock and Shutterstock

Manufactured in the United States of America

First Edition July 2017

To Lisa, whose love for The Men of At-Ease Ranch helped make the series such a success! You will be sorely missed!

And to the readers who wrote asking for more, I thank you from the bottom of my heart.

Chapter One

Hell must've frozen over.

Why else would she call? Zombie apocalypse? Storm damage from last week's tornado rampage? Something major had to happen for *her* to pick up the phone.

Cord Brannigan cut the engine to his truck in front of the tenacious woman's ranch and sat back to contemplate the irony of the situation. The very woman who put the I in independent had actually reached out for help on Independence Day.

His lips twitched into a rare grin. Probably pissed about it, too.

One thing was certain—she had to be desperate in order to call him, because Haley Wagner was as stubborn as she was beautiful.

He straightened in his seat. Thoughts like that led to nothing but trouble.

Haley was the widow of one of his Army Ranger buddies. Off-limits. A line he was never willing to cross, even in the two and a half years since his buddy's death.

Cord had ignored his attraction to the pretty brunette the whole time he'd served with Drew. He'd been unsuccessfully attending to Drew's wounds when his buddy had asked him to keep an eye on Haley.

"Tell her I love her. And I'm sorry. She deserved so much better. I need you to help her out. Keep an eye on her. Promise me, man. I need you to promise me you'll watch over her."

He'd promised, then Drew had let out a relieved breath… and died.

Shaking his head to clear the dark image from his mind, he stared out at the quiet ranch. Ever since he'd resigned his commission and left the military, Cord had done his best to fulfill his promise to Drew. Over the past two years, he came when Haley called, which wasn't often. And though he and the guys had tried to get her to visit At-Ease a few times, she'd always politely declined. It was as if she needed to put distance between them and the other veterans living on the ranch in order to get on with her life. Understandable. They respected her wishes as much as possible. He still had his promise to keep to Drew, though. That would never change. He gave his word. His word was gold…unlike other's he'd known.

Discontent rippled through Cord's gut. He shifted in his seat with a muffled curse. That shit was in the past, and he was here to help Haley. She was a good person. Reliable. Honest. Maybe a little mouthy. His lips twitched. He kind of liked her sarcasm. But, without knowing it, she had the right idea. Given their unacknowledged attraction, distance was a good thing. He'd do well to remember that, especially considering he didn't know how the hell long he was here. Or why.

Cord scanned the large rambling one-story ranch and found nothing amiss. Two years ago, he and the guys had repaired and re-shingled the roof. Last spring, they'd shored up the long front porch, and last fall, he'd addressed a minor plumbing issue. The house wasn't the reason he was summoned. Had to be something else. He transferred his gaze across the driveway. There were two large barns, one old, and one…new? With an indoor arena attached?

Was that why was he there?

The answer would hopefully be forthcoming since the old barn door opened and Haley appeared with her arms full of blankets piled so high the woman could barely see over them. And now, with her view obstructed, she was heading right for a tractor left out in the yard.

Jesus.

Cord was out of the truck and sprinting toward her in a shot, concern ripping through his gut. "Haley…watch out!"

He made it in front of her just in time for her to plow into him instead of the tractor.

"Oh!"

Several blankets fell at their feet, while a few others were squished between them as he banded his arms around her tight to keep them both from falling.

"Cord! Where in the world did you come from? Thin air? Another dimension?" She drew back and shook her head, her ponytail swishing while the brown gaze that teased his dreams in the long hours of the night sparked with annoyance. "I didn't hear you pull up."

"I can tell."

"Gee, what gave it away?" She snorted. "The fact I was minding my own business before you blindsided me? Or because I nearly mowed you over?" she asked as she retrieved her lost blankets. "Your Ranger nickname should've been Ninja. Or Stealth Bomber."

He thought about pointing out that if he hadn't appeared, she would've been sporting a few injuries from her imminent collision with the tractor behind him, but he kept his mouth shut and swiped the last two blankets from the ground by his feet.

"I appreciate you coming," she said, looking a little more harried than he'd expected.

She was a strong, capable woman with a wicked sense of humor and a killer smile…which had been MIA the past two years.

Ever since Drew had died.

His gut twisted.

He straightened with the blankets under his arm. "What's going on here?"

The place seemed deserted. No ranch hands or livestock. Just two brand new buildings and an old one in need of repair.

And weeds. A shit-ton of weeds.

It wasn't like her ranch hand Pete to let the place go like this. The old timer's truck was parked near his cabin in the distance, but there was no movement there, either.

"Come in the house and I'll tell you about it over something cold. I'm thirsty," she said, walking around him, and nearly smacked the tractor anyway. She stiffened and turned to face him, color flooding her cheeks…and she smiled.

God, she had the greatest smile. It warmed her brown eyes to the color of perfectly aged whiskey. Both exquisite. Two things he hadn't had the privilege of enjoying in years.

"That's why you ran into me," she said, nodding toward the tractor. "I'm sorry for biting your head off. Very ungracious of me. Thanks for the quick save."

Technically she ran into him, but he was never one to cast stones. Besides, his mind was still in the stupor realm from her damn smile, and now she was being nice and apologizing. What the hell was he supposed to do with that?

The one and only time he'd given himself permission to react to a pretty girl with a pretty smile had ended in disaster, so from then on he'd kept things simple and physical.

Clearing his throat, he lifted a shoulder and nodded. "You're welcome."

As soon as he uttered them, Cord realized it had been years since he'd spoken those words. *Why?* he wondered with a start. They were simple, common courtesy words.

Christ. When the hell had he turned into a damn ogre?

And as he followed his host up to the house, he tried to concentrate on that thought and not how well Haley's jeans fit her sweet ass, or the fact her tank top was riding up to expose a smooth expanse of skin.

Did it feel as soft as it looked?

"It does," she was saying, bringing his attention back to the conversation. "I know. But, I'll get to it. It's on my to-do list."

Since his mind had been on her body and not her words, he had no idea what she was adding to her list. He'd figure that out later. He stepped out onto the porch and reached around her to open the door, but he didn't get out of the way quick enough to avoid the brush of her curves as she passed.

The current he felt zipping in the air around them solidified in that split second, and a heated energy shot through his whole body, waking every single muscle at once.

Even the long dormant one.

"Thank you," she said, her voice a little breathless.

That dormant muscle reacted to the soft sound as if stroked.

Ah hell.

Not trusting his voice, he nodded then followed her into the blessedly cool air-conditioned house her uncle had left her after he passed away.

She's changed since she inherited the ranch. Drew's words echoed in Cord's head.

He wasn't sure if it was the ranch or his buddy's passing, but Haley *was* different now. The funny, vivacious force of nature he remembered meeting for the first time when Drew had introduced his wife to the team four years ago was but a memory. Life happened. He got that. Hell, he was certainly not the same guy he'd been back then, either. Shit happened. Then more shit. And although he prided himself on rolling with the punches, he wasn't sure he had the ability to block much more.

It'd been one of the reasons he'd decided to retire from the Army. He always heard a soldier knew when to retire. Well, he'd known. So had the rest of the team.

What was left of them.

"You can just place the blankets on the chair," Haley told him, setting her armful down. "I'll get them in the wash after I show you your room, and we'll have a drink."

His room.

He'd packed an overnight bag when she'd called a few hours ago, but something in her tone just now made it sound as if his help was needed a little longer. A mystery he hadn't been able to solve by the time she'd shown him his room and they returned to the open concept kitchen for that drink.

"I appreciate you coming on such short notice." She set an iced tea in front of him before sitting down with a glass of lemonade.

Even though it had been years since they'd sat down together she still remembered his drink preference. Despite his efforts to block the warm feeling spreading through his chest, Cord tried to ignore it. He came there to work. Not socialize. Or connect with her.

"Where's Pete? The place is a mess." Damn, that came out gruff.

He could tell it didn't go unnoticed by the way Haley's back stiffened and what little bit of civility that'd been present in her gaze had frosted over.

"I'm doing the best I can."

Christ, he had shit for brains. The few cells that remained. Damn woman messed with his mind whenever she was near.

He thought he'd had a handle on it, but she was single now and that made her dangerous, and his body was ignoring the off-limits warning from his head.

...

Haley Wagner tried to hold onto her smile, but the sexy jerk had to ruin it.

Leave it to her late husband's friend to spark life into her body only to suck it away the second he opened his sexy damn mouth.

That was so like Cord. The rare times he'd been to the ranch since he'd retired, she either wanted to punch him, or press him against a damn wall to kiss him until they were both ready to pass out from lack of oxygen.

She opted for neither.

If she hadn't needed his help so damn bad, she would've shared her drink with his face. But that was childish, and a waste of good homemade lemonade. Took her ten minutes to hand squeeze the lemons, and the damn juice burned the small cuts on her fingers from cleaning out the barn.

No sense in suffering through all of that to waste the efforts on his face. Besides, she'd have to clean up the floor, so it'd only create more work for her. That would be dumb. And she wasn't dumb.

Neither was he.

Haley had no idea what it was about Cord Brannigan, but he always got her hackles up. She'd hoped a few years away from the military would've mellowed the guy.

As if.

The tightlipped, stern-faced, lean-bodied Texan appeared even harder now, both in body and demeanor. And, dammit, if it didn't up his allure. The body she could appreciate; her good parts were already on alert. The lack of manners, not so much.

Regardless of his temperament, though, those gorgeous green eyes of his mesmerized and pulled her in, made her want things she had no business wanting.

Besides, who's to say she'd hold his interest, anyway? He was a virile man like Drew, and she hadn't held his.

"Sorry." He blew out a breath and ran a hand through his hair, having the good grace to appear contrite. "I didn't mean it like it sounded. Pete's meticulous. So something must've happened to him."

Observant as ever. "Warlock," as the team called him, had powers of deduction that couldn't be faulted. She'd give him that. Cord always had the ability to size up a situation—or a person—with just one glance. It was the main reason she'd avoided the guys and their ranch, despite their many invites. Not that she wasn't interested or proud of their efforts to create a place for veterans to transition into society, she just felt a damn attraction to Cord she did not want or need. And she sure as hell didn't need him to catch on, as he undoubtedly would if they were in each other's orbit for too long.

But she needed help, and the guy had made her promise to call if she did, so she called. He arrived three hours later.

"Pete fell off the barn roof and broke his leg," she replied with a shudder, remembering the accident vividly. Thank God that was all he'd broken. It could've been a lot worse.

"Jesus." Cord's head snapped back. "Is he all right? Pete has to be pushing seventy."

A smile tugged her lips despite the solemnness of the conversation. Damn man was too astute. "Pete turns seventy in September. And yes, he's okay. Pissed off because he can't do anything around here—not that he doesn't try." She had her hands full preventing her friend from complicating his injury further. "Thankfully, his sister is driving down from Dallas tomorrow to take him back home with her for a few weeks."

He nodded. "Too tempting for him to do something foolish if he stayed."

"Exactly." Her insides fluttered. It was weird. His words had felt like a premonition for the two of them.

"So, where is everyone?"

She sipped her lemonade and shrugged. "I let them go."

"Go?" His gaze narrowed. "Why?"

"Couldn't afford them or the cattle," she replied, ready with a retort if he made a rash comment about her being stupid.

She knew she was. Didn't need him to tell her. She was well aware of her shortcomings. It was her fault the ranch failed. She'd been too trusting. Too blind. Tenacity rushed through her veins and stiffened her backbone. Well, not anymore.

Not ever again.

"So, why did you build a new barn and arena?" Curiosity filled his gorgeous green gaze, without any signs of condemnation.

She regarded him closely. "I'm turning this place into a horse boarding ranch."

His chin lifted while his gaze continued to bore deep. Then he nodded. "Seems feasible. You have the space, and there isn't one in this area, to my knowledge."

"There isn't." She'd checked into that and all aspects of the venture over the past year. "I sold off the cattle and put up the new buildings. Now, I need to finish fixing the old barn, build an outdoor arena and two more corrals."

His brows rose. "And you need this done when?"

The sooner the better. Money was tight. "Three weeks."

He muttered an oath before drinking his tea.

"Look, I don't expect you to stay here that long," she rushed to say, and her chest squeezed tight. "I know you have your own ranch to run and business to operate. As a matter of fact, I didn't expect you to rush here so soon. I feel bad drawing you away from all that."

He set his glass down and shrugged. "The guys can handle the slack, so don't sweat it."

"Then what was the cursing for?" Damn man was so hard to read.

"The tight timeframe," he replied. "Is there a reason it's so short?"

She nodded. "Word has gotten out and I've already been approached by a few key people in the county to board their horses. I don't want them looking elsewhere, so when they asked if I'd be ready by August, of course I said yes. My lawyer is taking care of the licensing and permits." But there was still so much to do. She expelled a breath, willing the stars to align in her favor this time.

"I'll make it happen." His gaze almost warmed. "Don't worry."

Just when she had him shoved in that "jerk" category, he went and said something sweet. She cleared her throat and nodded because he seemed to be waiting for her reaction. "Thanks. I appreciate any time you can give me."

"You hiring the people who did the new buildings?"

Her laughter echoed between them, sounding hollow even to her ears. It was laughable how he thought she had money. Not that she blamed him. She was a war widow, so of course, he'd naturally assume she was beneficiary to her husband's death benefits.

She was not.

Not solely, anyway.

And she was certainly not going to talk to him about it. So, she answered as truthful as possible. "No. It's just you and me. But I do have people scheduled to build the outdoor arena once we get the fences up."

He finished the remainder of his drink in one gulp then set his glass down on the table with a *thud*. "I can stay 'til

August if you need me. Why don't we go outside so you can walk me through your plans?"

Good idea. Sitting here, making normal conversation, was having an adverse effect on her body and mind, causing her to consider he was almost human.

Living under the same roof was bad enough when they were barely civil, but if they were actually friendly?

That was way too dangerous a concept.

Chapter Two

The following morning, Cord was replacing the head gasket on the tractor, having discovered that was the reason it sat useless in a lawn of weeds, when his phone rang.

He wiped his hands on a rag then set it on the tractor before answering his phone.

"Hey, Cord," Brick greeted. "Sorry I missed your call last night. I was…uh…otherwise occupied."

Christ, for eight damn hours? His stomach rolled, knowing what his buddy had been doing and to whom. Cord's sister.

"So, you two haven't killed each other yet?" Amusement dripped from the guy's tone.

"Yeah, she killed me with sarcasm. You're talking to my ghost."

Jackass.

"Ha-ha. Well, I did get your texts this morning and filled the others in on your shack up…I mean stay."

Cord clenched his jaw. He didn't need this crap. "You getting to a point soon?"

"Yeah, just wanted to bust your hump and tell you not to

worry about your crew. Leo will take over."

He nodded as if his buddy could see him. Leo had made huge strides over the past few months. "Sounds good."

"Yep. So…"

Cord heard whispering on the other end.

"Your sister wants to know if the chemistry is still there."

He answered by hitting end and shoving the phone back in his pocket. Last thing he was about to do was talk to anyone about any chemistry he may or may not have with Haley. Especially since, yeah, they definitely still had chemistry.

"I thought that was you, Cord." Old Pete hobbled toward him on crutches while trying to carry a bottle of water. "Good to see you again. Got time to take a break?" The man halted to wave the bottle.

"Sure do." He stepped forward to take the water in one hand and shake the ranch manager's hand with other. "How's the leg?"

Pete snorted. "Hurts like the dickens." The older man had come with the property, and from what Cord could remember, the guy had worked for Haley's uncle for decades. The seasoned manager knew everything about the ranch and ranching, so she'd kept him on.

"Hang on, I'll grab a folding chair from inside the barn," he said.

"No, don't bother. Thanks." Pete shook his head as he carefully leaned back against the tractor and sighed. "I need to stand. Been sitting for the past week now. Can't feel my ass."

Cord chuckled, twisting the cap off the bottle, then stilled. "Did you say week?"

Pete nodded. "Yeah. It'll be a week tomorrow."

"And Haley didn't call me until yesterday?" He muttered a curse, then washed the rest down with the remainder of the water.

Damn stubborn woman.

The old timer chuckled. "Yeah, because I told her I wasn't going to go with my sister if she didn't call you and the others."

An invisible weight hit Cord's chest. Jesus, what if Pete hadn't pushed her into calling? Was she seriously going to try to tackle all this on her own?

"Yep," the guy replied as if reading Cord's mind. "She's stubborn, that one. Thinks she's invincible, too. But she needs to slow down. Been burning the candle at both ends for over three years now. Working her ass off to make a go of it when she first inherited the place. And was succeeding, too, until her husband messed things up."

Cord's heart dropped to his boots, and he eyed the man closely, trying to gauge if he'd meant when Drew died, or had his buddy screwed something up here beforehand? "What do you mean?"

Pete blinked, and a look of disgust soured his face. "Oh hell, Cord. Don't pay me no mind. I don't mean to be talking ill of the dead. That pain med they have me on is making me goofy."

Fuck. Drew *did* do something to screw with the place, and left Haley to deal with it.

"Tell her I love her. And I'm sorry. She deserved so much better…"

His buddy's final words rushed through his head.

"And besides, Haley's got things going in a good direction again. I'm just glad you'll be around to lend her a hand before she drops from exhaustion. She's too hard on herself. Between the sacrifices and the workload, she's close to pushing it too far."

He nodded, unsure what to say, so he remained quiet. Whenever the Rangers were between missions, Drew and Haley were always jet setting off to one exotic locale after another, trying out new equipment or checking out new destinations for her job as a travel blogger for an outdoor magazine. His buddy told him that was how the two had met. On a rafting adventure. She'd joined the group in order to write an article about the adventure, and Drew had been there for the adrenaline rush.

"At least I know you won't be afraid to put your foot down and make her pace herself." Fondness softened the man's weathered face when his gaze shifted to the house. Haley was inside, meeting with people from the local 4-H club to discuss activities for the youth, and the possibility of hiring a few to help out.

A brilliant idea that sent a surge of pride through his chest in a warm rush.

"She's eager to get the venture going, not just to get money coming in again, but to have horses on the ranch again, too. I know she misses Gypsy."

Cord stilled, as it dawned on him that all the barns were empty. He glanced at Pete. "What happened to her horse?" On past visits, he'd seen the woman's tough shell disappear around the prized mustang she'd adopted from a rescue auction a few years back.

"She had to sell her, too." Pete's voice turned wispy. "I swear, Cord. It just about killed her. But she had bills to pay and payroll to meet at the time, so she did what she's always done. Put others' needs before her own."

He could relate, and because of that his insides hollowed at the thought of her sacrificing the horse she'd bonded with after her uncle's death. It confused the hell out of him.

Why was she hurting that bad for money?

It wasn't something he and the guys used to like to think about, but they knew if they'd been killed in action, their loved ones would've been taken care of financially. They'd be comfortable, and depending on their debt at the time, possibly pretty well off.

So why wasn't Haley?

She had to sell her damn horse. What the hell?

Before he could ask, the door opened, and Haley and the 4-H people stepped onto the porch, smiling and shaking hands.

"Looks like that went well," Pete noted.

As soon as they got in their cars and drove off in a cloud of dust, Haley squealed and dashed over to where he and Pete stood. The smile on her lips was one of her rare, brilliant, *genuine* smiles. The kind capable of reaching into his soul with a warm, bright light.

"Did that just happen?" she asked, disbelief mixing with hope in the gaze she flicked between them.

Pete grinned. "You bet. You get the 4-H behind your idea to hire out some of the kids?"

She practically bounced on the balls of her feet. "They'll present it at their meeting in two weeks, but I think they'll go for it."

Pete patted her shoulder. "You're going to make a lot of kids very happy. It's a great opportunity you're giving them."

"I would've loved it at their age." A shadow fell across her expression. "Of course, I was never in one place long enough to join. But I'm excited for them, and me."

Her smile was back, but Cord's mind snagged on her words. They implied she'd had upheaval in her childhood. Something he could relate to, and it strengthened their bond.

Damn.

That was the last thing he needed, especially with Pete about to leave them completely alone. Last night, she took supper over to the man at his cabin and stayed there to eat with him. Cord had declined her invitation to join them, opting to eat alone in the house. Not that he didn't like Pete, he just didn't want to socialize with Haley any more than necessary.

Now that buffer was about to leave.

A car pulled up the drive, and the older man straightened from his perch. "That'd be my sister."

Haley leaned in to kiss his cheek. "You take it easy," she ordered, drawing back. "I need you healed up."

Pete grinned. "Yes, ma'am. And I need you to listen to Cord. Don't overdo it. Let him help."

"I will."

Pete narrowed his gaze. "Promise me, Haley."

He noted the guy had a bit of stubbornness, too. Which he probably needed in order to deal with Haley on a day-to-day basis.

"I promise," she insisted. "That's why I called him."

The old man turned to him and held out his hand. "I feel better knowing you're here. Thanks for coming."

"Of course." He set his hand on the guy's back and nodded. "Everything will be fine. Including Haley. You worry about yourself."

Relief was evident on the man's face as he got in the car. Cord wondered if it was relief to be leaving, or because someone was there to keep an eye on Haley and the ranch. He stood contemplating the answer as he watched the car disappear down the drive.

Haley turned to him and nodded toward the tractor. "How's it coming?"

"Good," he replied. "I just finished replacing the head gasket with one I picked up in town this morning." He hadn't wanted to wake her and ask about accounts or money, so he happily paid for it out of his pocket. It was better than the alternative—waking her up and seeing her in her pajamas. He wouldn't put it past the woman to sleep in the nude. Christ. He couldn't handle that. Not when he'd want to literally handle her.

Her gaze fell to his chin and she grinned. "You have grease smeared on you." She stepped close, and before he knew it, she grabbed the rag off the tractor and proceeded to wipe his face.

His whole body went on red alert. She was so close he could see the caramel flecks in her chocolate brown eyes. So close, they shared a breath, which suddenly stopped when her gaze lifted to his.

"Sorry, I…" she whispered, her voice disappearing on a hitched breath.

Cord fought like hell to keep his gaze from her mouth, but he lost the battle early on and stared at the full lips he'd wanted to kiss for years. Even though the temperature was already a hundred degrees and hot as hell, the air around them heated further with an electric intensity he'd never experienced. It was insane. And dangerous. And he needed her to move. Reaching out to grasp her upper arms, he intended to push her away, but the wires in his messed up brain got crossed and he started to pull her closer instead. Blood *whooshed* through his veins on its journey south, and his mouth hovered above hers, anticipation stirring fires he hadn't wanted to start.

Then her palms brushed his shoulders, and that little show of acceptance did him in.

He moved in to take her lips—

The phone in his pocket rang, startling him back to reality and halting his stupidity.

What the hell was he doing?

Uttering a curse, he released her stiffening body and stepped back, noting a measure of relief entering her gaze. "Yeah," he muttered into his phone without checking caller ID, grateful to whomever it was for helping him dodge a bullet.

It was one of his partners, and as Stone updated him on the construction job he left in order to help Haley, Cord watched her nod before heading for the barn. An unwanted flash of disappointment swept through him.

He was an ass. That was way too close a call. It was going to take all his training to resist their damn attraction.

...

That evening, Haley was still mad at herself for being weak. She'd almost kissed Cord. What was she thinking?

She wasn't. That was the problem. Whenever she got near the man, her brain shut down and her body took over. Stupid body. Damn traitor. Cord was off limits. He was one of Drew's military brothers. The Ranger Rifle Team had been tight. They'd fought and bled together. Protected one another. Respected one another. She refused to take that away from them by falling under Cord's spell and losing the brain capacity to keep the truth about Drew to herself.

So why the hell did she keep thinking about that single, brief moment in time with his callus-roughened hands on her bare arms and his delectable mouth practically brushing hers?

Because she was an idiot, that's why. And he was hot as hell and haunted her deepest secret fantasies for the past two years.

But as soon has his phone rang, it not only snapped her back to reality, it snapped him back, too. The censure in his green eyes told her he didn't want the attraction, either.

That should've made her feel better. It was an extra safeguard should her control slip again. Except, if that phone call hadn't happened, Haley knew with utmost certainty they would've kissed. Their desire to resist the attraction would've turned into just plain desire.

Dammit.

That wasn't a comforting thought. There was still a good two weeks or more worth of work to do in order to meet her August deadline. She needed Cord. Sending him away wasn't an option. And he said he'd stay the whole time. Resisting him was her only recourse, so she was just going to have to keep her distance and treat him like a worker.

Which would not be easy tonight, considering they were about to sit down to supper in her kitchen. Alone.

Her mind raced to find the answer to her strange behavior. For years now, she was steadfast and certain. Strong in her convictions. Not frivolous. Work was important, whether it was running a cattle ranch or building a horse boarding ranch. All her attention stayed in work mode.

After Drew's betrayal, she hadn't had sex, let alone thought about it, other than her secret Cord fantasies. But fantasizing about the man and actually engaging in the act were two very different things.

Her stomach hollowed out. If her husband had gone looking elsewhere, she had to be lacking in that department. Cord was way out of her league. Just because a few sparks had flown between them didn't mean she'd hold his interest in bed.

She heard the shower shut off and her attention quickly shifted to thoughts of toweling off the wet, naked muscles of one lean, green-eyed, gorgeous man in her bathroom. Damn. What happened to her strong, steadfast convictions? Or the unease of her inadequacies?

They were too busy making room for the desire flooding her body.

With a muffled oath, she quickly stepped to the sink to peel a cucumber so she wouldn't be tempted to glance down the hall when he emerged to head to his room.

Her pulse hiccupped at the thought. She did not need to see any part of that man without clothes. When she heard his door shut, she set the cucumber on the counter and marched to the central air controls to see if it was on. It was suddenly very hot. Or maybe it was just her. Yeah, probably just her.

She drew in a deep breath then expelled it slowly,

regaining her calm as she finished the salad and checked on the chicken roasting in the oven. Almost done. Like her. She was almost ready to face the evening.

For most of the day, they managed to avoid each other. Cord spent the morning on the tractor, cutting the acreage until it got too hot, then he switched to working on stalls in the old barn. She stayed in the new one, setting up the tack room.

One thing was certain, there was plenty to do to keep them occupied and out of each other's orbit. Two days down, nineteen to go.

She was placing the bowl of salad on the table next to the mashed potatoes when he entered the kitchen and stopped dead.

"I hope you didn't cook anything for me," he said, concern darkening his gaze. "I have to run into town to grab a few things for tomorrow, and then head to my mom's. She heard I was only an hour away and insisted I have dinner with her and my grandmother tonight."

Disappointment and relief raced through Haley's body at the same time. She straightened up and faced him. "No worries. I can turn the leftovers into chicken salad for our lunch tomorrow. Go visit with your mom." She'd give anything to have dinner with her mom, but a fatal car accident took away that possibility ten years ago.

He hesitated, glancing from the table to her. "You sure? I can call—"

"I'm sure," she cut him off and smiled. "Go ahead. Enjoy your visit."

Of course, it would've been nice to know before she'd made them dinner. Typical male. They thought women were mind readers. At least now she didn't have to worry about eating while tense.

"Sorry. I didn't think to tell you," he said. "I'm an ass."

She waved a hand at him. "You didn't need to tell me. I already knew you were an ass."

He was smiling as he walked out the door.

She was smiling, too. The man had the best grin. Shaking her head to clear out the Cord stupor, she removed the chicken from the oven and set it on the table for one. Now, maybe she'd at least be able to taste the food without that attraction in the air to mess with her mind.

Was this what she had to look forward to?

If so, it was going to be a tough three weeks.

Chapter Three

Cord still felt bad about dinner the night before. He'd been so busy trying to avoid the woman yesterday that he didn't think to tell her about his dinner plans. It had never crossed his mind that she'd cook for him. He was there to help, not cause her more work.

And yet, here she was setting a heaping plate of eggs and bacon in front of him.

"Thanks, but you really don't have to be cooking for me," he said, already knowing she was a good cook, having sat down to dinner with her and Drew and the rest of the guys a few times in the past. Even Vince, their resident cook, approved.

She smiled. "It's the least I can do, since you won't let me pay you for your help. Besides, I'm cooking for myself anyway. It's no biggie to cook for two."

He nodded and dug in, enjoying the quiet that settled over the table. It was so peaceful on her ranch. First thing that morning, he sat on the porch with his coffee and watched the sun rise. It'd been years since he'd experienced that kind of calm. He was already looking forward to a repeat tomorrow morning.

"So, what are your plans today?" she asked, halfway through breakfast.

He finished his orange juice and set the glass down. "Cut more weeds until I start to bake, then switch to working in the barn again. Why? Did you need something specific done?"

She shook her head. "No. Whatever you do will be fine. And don't forget, there's chicken salad in the fridge, so help yourself when you get hungry."

He nodded, remorse setting in once more. "Sorry, again, about last night."

"It's okay." She even smiled. "But do you have any more plans I should know about?"

"None tonight. I'll be here," he told her. "But not tomorrow night, so don't include me in your dinner plans. As a matter of fact, I won't be back until the next morning."

Something unreadable passed through her eyes before she nodded. "Will do. Thanks for telling me."

He contemplated skipping the weekly group therapy session held at At-Ease, but each time more and more soldiers wandered in and took part. Some even opened up when he and the other guys from his Ranger team took the floor.

Not his favorite thing to do, same as his friend Brick, but they understood their participation helped others. That was the reason he and his three buddies had opened the transition ranch in the first place.

Besides, it also got him away from being alone with Haley, and the elephant in the room—their attraction. Damn thing was gaining strength the more time they spent together.

Like now.

The temperature around them had significantly increased when she sat down across from him. Not good. In fact, it was bad. He concentrated on his food, making small talk when prompted, then left as soon as he finished eating.

Once outside, he could breathe and think. Two of his favorite things to do. Neither were his number one favorite, though. No, that was exactly what he was trying to avoid.

The key was keeping busy, and hell, there was certainly enough to keep him busy around her ranch. In fact, there was *too* much, but Haley didn't need to know.

Doing his best to put the sexy woman out of his mind, he climbed on the tractor and considered the workload while cutting the far pasture. He was going to have to tap the guys to pitch in a day here and there, or bring his team of workers in for a day once their latest job was done.

Foxtrot Construction, the company he and his buddies also owned, employed veterans. And like each of his partners, he supervised a four-man crew. They'd kick ass here. It would speed up the progress and get him the hell away from temptation that much sooner.

A minute from becoming a crisp piece of bacon, Cord headed back to the barn, unable to put it off any longer. The day's chores filled his head, and he breathed easier. It was a safe bet he wouldn't see her until sundown.

As soon as he cut the engine outside the barn, he heard a large crash from inside followed by a slew of curses.

Haley.

With his gut knotted tight, he crossed the yard and entered on a sprint. "Haley…Jesus," he muttered, finding her underneath a pegboard and a pile of tools. Sharp ones. Shit.

"*Now* you show up," she scoffed.

He hoisted the peg board and tossed it aside. "What the hell happened?"

"Had a fight with a wall and lost." A smirk twitched her full lips and gleamed in her whiskey gaze.

"That's not funny."

"Damn straight." She frowned. "It hurts like a bitch."

He ran a hand through his hair. "How the hell did you manage to knock this over?"

"Quite well, actually."

Smart-ass.

He knelt beside her and leveled his gaze on her. "That's not what I meant, and you know it."

"Did I?" She tipped her chin and narrowed her eyes. "Hard to tell underneath all that accusation and condemnation dripping from your tone. I'm not one of your Rangers, *Warlock*. That hard stare of yours won't work on me."

Christ. He didn't need this shit.

She made to get up, pushing a few tools out of the way, and that's when he noticed the blood dripping down her arm.

"Stay still," he ordered, grasping her unharmed arm to hold her steady. "Let me have a look."

A quick inspection deemed it deep but not stitch-worthy, thank God. He yanked off his shirt and wrapped it around her arm, ignoring her gasp as he tied it tight until he could get her in the house for some proper first aid. But he didn't want her moving until he examined the rest of her body for injuries.

With his training kicking in, he ran his hands over her, noting a small cut on her cheek, another on the back of her hand, and a bruise on her other wrist, no doubt from covering her face.

"You okay?" he asked, staring into her dazed eyes. "Are you hurt anywhere else?"

She blinked and focused her gaze on his face, then shook her head after she opened her mouth and nothing came out.

Christ.

His insides twisted when he took in the mash of clippers, hammers, screwdrivers, and pliers scattered around them. She was lucky. So damn lucky.

After helping her to her feet, he bent to scoop her in his arms.

"W-what are you doing?" She wiggled as he carried her across the yard, trying his damndest not to notice the soft curves brushing his chest.

"Taking you inside to fix your arm. Stay still." Awareness already spread through his body, waking up parts that had no business enjoying the feel of his dead friend's widow cradled against him.

Haley grunted. "I can walk."

"Good to know," he replied, but continued to hold her as he stepped onto the porch. "Get the door."

With a loud sigh, she reached out and twisted the knob. "Okay, you can put me down now."

"Where's your first-aid kit?" he asked, ignoring her protests.

She closed her mouth and stared at him, her eyes twin pools of pissed-off brown. God, she was gorgeous. And damn, he did not need to have his arms full of her hot curves.

He muttered an oath. "You can keep quiet all you want, but I'm just going to stand here and hold you until you tell me."

Even if it killed him.

"Fine," she grumbled. "It's in the bathroom under the sink."

With a nod, he headed in that direction, happy to have a destination. Once inside, he set her gently on the counter, then bent to retrieve the kit.

Images of the op that went horribly wrong, and the fallout that followed, flashed through Cord's mind. His inability to save his teammate and the innocent little girl from the local village had haunted him ever since. That day haunted all of them.

He'd only cracked open a first-aid kit one time since.

"You okay?" she asked quietly. "You've gone awfully still."

Silently cursing his weakness and the fact she'd spotted it, he grabbed the kit and straightened. "I'm good." And he meant it. There was no way in hell he wouldn't help Haley. She was hurt. So even if he hadn't popped his cherry treating Brick's injuries this past spring, Cord would still be standing in front of her ready to come to her aid.

It was Haley. That changed everything. She was the exception. The exception to every rule.

That realization scared the hell out of him.

...

Haley watched Cord gently unwrap his shirt and peer at her wound. Never in a million years would she ever forget the sight of him yanking the shirt over his head one-handed to use it for a tourniquet on her cut.

The man literally gave her the shirt off his back.

Drew would've used *her* shirt. She gave herself a mental shake. He had nothing to do with this. He was in her past.

Cord was here. He was the one taking care of her.

Her stomach fluttered. No one had ever done anything like that for her. She vaguely remembered gasping, but it had nothing to do with her wound and everything to do with the sight of Cord's broad chest and tightly muscled abs and biceps. Then he'd picked her up and held her against them.

The urge to melt into him had been so strong she'd needed to get him to put her down. Purgatory and ecstasy yanked her in opposite directions. Even now, her tongue remained swollen and her gaze kept straying over his lean tanned form. He was gorgeous.

"Doesn't need stitching. But this is going to sting," he warned, disinfecting the cut, and when she muttered a curse, he leaned close and blew on the wound.

Awareness spread through her body in a wave of tingling

heat, and her heart cracked open at his thoughtful gesture. It was as shocking as it was sensuous. The big bad Ranger with the hot, hard body had a soft side she hadn't expected. Haley curled her fingers around the counter to keep from reaching for him.

You're just his patient, it'll be over soon, she chanted in her head each time he disinfected and treated a cut. Her gaze remained on his fingers, watching as he peeled back the plastic packaging on the sterilized bandages and covered the wound on her arm, and then the one on her hand.

"You were the field medic, right?" she asked, noting he stilled for a brief second.

"Yes."

He didn't elaborate so she didn't push. Somewhere in the recesses of her mind she remembered he'd been with Drew when he'd died. Cord had passed on a message to her during that nightmare of a time. She'd been saddened by her husband's death, but not devastated. No. That had happened a few months earlier when she found out Drew had cheated on her. More than once.

When Cord finished with the cut on her hand, he lifted the other one, rotating it gently to probe the swollen area.

She cleared her throat. "It's okay. It's not broken. Just bruised."

He nodded, and while he concentrated on his task of expertly wrapping it with an Ace bandage, she studied his face. It was tense and edgy and gorgeous. She'd never been this close to him before. His jaw was strong, with the barest impression of a divot in the center, and heaven help her, she had the strongest urge to lean in and lick it.

A delicious shiver raced down her body and increased at the thought of brushing against his days' worth of scruff. Mmm…she could only imagine how incredible that rough jaw would feel scraping against her skin. Good Lord, she was pathetic.

And sexually freaking frustrated.

It explained her inability to control her thoughts and reactions around Cord. But what pent-up woman wouldn't react this way toward a deliciously ripped, half-naked man standing between her legs?

Doing her best to quell her unwelcomed, out-of-control libido, she continued to take advantage of her close proximity to the enigma. There was a tiny scar along one side of his jaw, and he had dimples in his cheeks whenever he decided to smile, which wasn't nearly enough.

"Do you miss active duty, Cord?"

"Not really." He shrugged. "I like what I'm doing now."

He finished with her wrist, then turned his attention to her face. Her heart rocked in her chest, then hammered in her ears as his fingers lightly brushed her cheek.

She clenched her jaw to keep from whispering his name. Lordy, she was acting like a virgin. Cripes. It wasn't like she'd never been touched before. Hell, she'd been married. And until she'd discovered her husband's infidelity, they'd had a very healthy sex life. Or so she'd thought.

But Drew's touch had never prompted the type of reactions Cord's induced.

They were strong and special and unexpected. Much like the man.

While he dabbed disinfectant on her cheek, she stared at his broad shoulder, trying desperately to hold back a wince from the sting of antiseptic, and to avoid his gaze. That's when she noticed it. A light peppering of freckles. She transferred her gaze to the other side and her insides fluttered. Both shoulders sported the sexy flecks, and once again, she found herself swamped with the urge to lean in and lick the guy.

In an attempt to keep her cool, she tightened her grip on the counter and fought the urges rushing through her.

"You okay?" he asked.

No. No she wasn't. She was far from okay. "Yes," she replied instead, her voice barely above a whisper.

Then he blew on her cheek, and the warm air caressing her sensitized skin was too much. Just too freaking much for her poor lustful body to endure. A strangled whimper sounded in her throat.

Cord stilled for a brief second, then trailed his finger down her face to hook under her chin, urging her to look at him. "Haley," he murmured, his voice low and rough, sending goose bumps over her skin.

With butterflies swarming low in her belly, she met his gaze and noted several hues of green in his beautiful eyes. That was it. Everything outside of her rapidly beating heart and the man controlling her pulse disappeared, leaving them in a cocoon of heated need.

Then he let out a low growl and brought his mouth down on hers.

Chapter Four

Hungry and firm, Cord's lips gave and demanded without apology, and Haley wasn't sorry, either. She knew his mouth would be amazing on hers. She knew it and had fantasized about it for two years now, but...*holy shit, Sherlock*. She hadn't been prepared for the real deal. For raw Cord. Never expected his kiss to be this good.

So freaking good.

His tongue slipped inside and brushed against hers in a delicious show of need she matched without hesitation. God, she was swamped by new sensations. New urges. She'd never been kissed like there was nothing on earth more important than her. He made her feel soft and feminine, and desired above all others. It was amazing. And she needed that. Sweet mercy, she never realized how much she needed that.

Shoving her hands in his hair, she held his head and kissed him back with the same fierce enthusiasm, lost on this wild rush she never knew existed. Damn, the man could kiss. He was thorough, and hot, and very hungry.

Her hands ran over his magnificent body, brushing over

those sexy freckles and exploring the powerful muscles she'd lusted after in her dreams. His weren't dormant, either. He trailed a hand down her spine to palm one of her cheeks and tug her close. Heat rushed to all her quivering good parts, so when he suddenly stopped, released her and drew back, she uttered a protest and tried to clutch at him.

"Damn, Haley. I'm sorry," he muttered between breaths. "I shouldn't have done that…"

Before she could reply or even blink, he was gone, leaving her shaken to her core, wondering what the hell had just happened.

And whether his rejection was because he found her lacking, too…

...

The following evening, Cord was back at At-Ease, sitting in on the group therapy session held in the rec room in the back of the main house. A circle of folding chairs were set up for everyone to sit while one person talked about what troubled them. Most came to listen, some came to share. Tonight, Cord didn't do either. He zoned out. Completely flaked. His damn mind was in another county, at another ranch, holding a sexy woman in his arms, as he relived the hottest kiss he'd ever experienced.

Deep down, he always knew kissing Haley would be incredible, but damn, he hadn't expected the heat, or for her to be so responsive. One kiss had knocked him on his ass. She'd tasted unexpectedly sweet, like a ripe raspberry straight off the bush. And the way her curves had melted into him when she'd sighed released a fierce primal urge to protect, to worship, to have her for his very own.

What the bloody hell?

Luckily, a little brain matter had surfaced in time for him

to pull away when he had, otherwise…

Damn, he couldn't let his mind even think about *otherwise*.

"Cord, is there anything you'd like to say?" The therapist's voice broke through his confusion.

Other than he was an ass who needed to get his body under control? "No." He blinked the room back into focus and swallowed a curse when he found all eyes on him.

Ah hell. He was going to pay for it later. The Mitchum brothers had that look of knowing in their damn eyes.

"Then I guess we can call it a night. See you all next week." When the therapist stood, everyone else followed suit.

Cord got up, folded his chair, and carried it to where the others were stacking theirs, his mind focused on the beer that was calling his name from the refrigerator behind the bar. He felt bad—he usually tried to contribute to the sessions. The first few he'd shown up at were to support Leo, one of his fellow Rangers, who was the reason At-Ease and Foxtrot Construction became a reality.

Last year, Leo had tried to permanently quiet memories from the op that had landed the guy in the hospital and taken Drew's life. None of them came away unscathed, but Nikon—Leo—had a photographic memory, so the images never faded.

Christ, it ate at Cord's gut just thinking about his buddy's perpetual nightmare. Therapy was Leo's idea, and a good one. For months now, the guy had been going to private therapy and group with noticeable results.

Standing behind the bar, Cord cracked open his beer and watched Leo laugh at something Vince said as the two racked up a set of pool balls to start a game. The mood swings and alcohol binges seemed to be a thing of Leo's past.

Brick smirked, grabbing his own beer. "So tell me, Cord, are you enjoying playing house with Haley?"

Taller and a little wider than his brother, the good-looking jackass had earned the name Romeo for his prowess with the ladies. He'd earned Cord's friendship when they'd endured boot camp together, then came deployments, suffering through Ranger training, and finally, placement on the same Ranger Rifle Team. They went through hell and back multiple times, but nothing had ever tested their friendship until Brick started dating Cord's sister.

The idiot's only saving grace had been that he'd had no idea Beth was actually Cord's sister, Lizzie. Of course, Cord hadn't found out until after he'd defended his sister's honor and nearly ruined their relationship.

But it was all good now. And damn, he needed that drink. Putting the bottle to his lips, he tipped the beer back and let the ale wash away what ailed him. It didn't work.

"Yeah, Cord." Amusement crossed Vince's face. "I'd love to know the answer to that."

"Me, too." Stone sank down onto a bar stool on the other side of the counter, grabbing the beer Brick slid his way.

Shit. He was hoping by ignoring the question they'd let it drop.

Leo straightened from the table and leaned on the stick. "I noticed you packed a bigger bag. You moving in for good?"

"That's messed up," he said with a shake of his head, ignoring the twitch from the body part highly in favor of the idea.

"Why?" Brick frowned. "We were there, remember? Drew told you to take care of her."

Cord's gut soured. *Christ.* The guys had been too busy trying to help save Leo. Only Cord had heard the "she deserves better" in Drew's last breath. "He didn't mean it that way."

"Yes, he did," Brick insisted.

Vince nodded.

"Drew—" Stone began.

"Ah hell," he cut him off. "Not you, too." They didn't get it.

Nor did they realize by putting his wife first, their buddy had been unselfish for the first time in a long time. An attempt to make up for his betrayal. No way, no how, was he asking Cord to shack up with his wife.

Leo ambled closer. "I may have been busted up, but I can still see his face. He meant it, Cord. Drew needed to know you would be there for Haley. He gave his blessing."

Jesus, this was getting out of hand.

Cord exhaled. "That's exactly what I'm doing. She needs me to help her with a few things."

"I think you had the first part right." Brick slapped his back. "She needs *you*, buddy."

The jerks laughed in agreement. Cord stared them down.

"She needs all of us," he corrected, then went on to explain the woman's new venture. The deadline she was looking at earned a few curse words and worried looks.

"When you going back?" Stone asked.

"In the morning." He needed one more night to pull his head out of his ass and center himself. The past twenty-four hours since he lost his mind and kissed her had been a bit tense. Mostly his doing. He was the one who walked away and had been careful not to be in the same room with her since.

"Well, we're already scheduled out this weekend," Stone said, setting his beer on the bar, "but we should be able to finish up the Henderson job by Thursday. I don't see why Brick and I couldn't help you guys the next two weekends. Vince and Leo can handle things here."

Relief rushed through Cord. Between the three of them, they'd knock a lot off Haley's list.

Stone took a pull of his beer then pointed at his brother with the bottle. "I'm sure the girls would love to talk to Haley about the business side of boarding horses. We'll bring them, too."

Cord set his bottle on the counter and nodded. "Good."

It would be good for Haley to socialize. According to the guys, Lizzie and Jovy were enjoying a girls' night out. Haley needed that, too. From what he'd gathered from Pete, the woman hardly ever left the ranch, unless it was work related.

"So tell us, how is Haley?" Vince asked, standing back to let Leo shoot.

"Yeah." Brick smirked. "Has she loosened up any?"

He washed down a grunt with his last mouthful of beer. Yesterday, during that damn kiss, she'd been far from tight lipped. Her guard had dropped, loosening all sorts of feelings in him best left locked up tight.

"Still having trouble with your words, Cord?" Stone chuckled, lifting his bottle for another pull.

"Fuck you," he grunted.

Vince snickered. "No trouble with those words."

"So, you're saying the stubborn woman hasn't given you any trouble?" Brick glanced sideways at him, his eyes dark with disbelief. "She let you work? Didn't try to do things on her own?"

"Is she any good with tools?" Leo asked.

Cord tossed his empty bottle in the recycle bin in the corner and grabbed another beer from the fridge. "Yeah, she's good with them, especially on bringing them down on herself."

Leo frowned. "What? Tools fell on her?"

"Yeah." His chest tightened at the thought of the shears cutting her chest instead of her arm. She was damn lucky.

Stone straightened in his seat. "Was she hurt?"

He nodded. "Cut her arm and hand, and bruised her wrist. Not too bad, though. I took care of it."

Brick studied him closely. "Did you now?"

Christ. "Don't make a big deal out of it."

"But it *is* a big deal. Other than to fix my back, you haven't opened a first-aid kit in years."

He sipped his beer and shrugged. "She was bleeding. I couldn't just let her stand there and bleed."

"No," Stone said, "but you could've let Pete handle it."

Ah hell. He knew where this was going to lead. "Pete had already left to stay with his sister."

The whole room grew quiet. He swore the balls on the table even came to a complete stop.

Stone blinked. "Wait…didn't you say she let the other ranch hands go?"

"Yep."

"And she only kept Pete," Brick said.

"Yep."

"So it's just you and Haley on the ranch? Alone?" Vince asked, slight twitch to his lips.

Fuck it. He was done answering.

Brick folded his arms across his chest and continued to regard him closely. "And you're going to be there three weeks?"

He fought back his annoyance and lost. "So?"

"No *so*. None whatsoever." Brick shrugged. "But you, my friend…oh, you are so going down."

He jerked his head toward the idiot. "What the fuck are you talking about?

His buddy snorted. "You and Haley have killer chemistry, and now you're stuck in a house together all alone. Do the math, man."

"Changes nothing." Except it already had, and Jesus, if the guys ever found out he'd never hear the end of it. "Nothing is going to happen because I won't let it."

Brick and Stone glanced at each other before they barked out laughter loud enough Haley probably heard them in the next county.

Bastards. There wasn't anything funny about it.

He stared them down. Again. "When have you ever seen

me do anything I didn't want to?"

"Don't you see? That's just it. You *do* want to, Cord," Stone insisted. "You very much want to do stuff with Haley."

Brick clapped him on the shoulder. "We've been in your shoes, buddy."

He glanced at the others.

"Don't look at me," Leo said, holding up his hands. "I'm still working on getting my head on straight. Don't need to bring a woman into my shit."

God, could he relate.

Vince sighed, leaning on his stick. "I'd love to be in Stone and Brick's shoes."

"And what shoes are they?"

Brick grinned. "The 'I've got a handle on this attraction' shoes. Big news flash, pal. You don't." The idiot chuckled. "I felt the same way. Well, actually, ever since meeting your sister, I wanted to do stuff with her. To her. You get the picture."

Christ. Now he needed to wash his ears out with icepicks and rinse with a Japanese sai.

Brick grabbed his beer. "But I never planned for it to lead to a relationship."

Thank the Lord the guy was going to shut up. He didn't need to hear anything related to his sister and sex. Tipping back his bottle, he sucked down more beer.

"Yeah." Stone nodded, twisting his bottle on the counter. "You think, okay, I can handle a couple of dates. After all, it's only for a few weeks."

"Then bam." Brick hit his fist off his palm. "You don't want it to end."

"And you're left scrambling because you've fucked up."

"Big time."

He still didn't see what this had to do with him, though, and he was past tired of the subject. Time to end it. "Good talk." He finished off his second beer, tossed the empty bottle in the recycling bin, and nodded as he walked around the front of the bar. "Good night."

"You know what? For us, it will be." Stone grinned. "And you want to know why?"

"No."

"I'm going to tell you anyway." The bastard grinned. "Because we took a chance and let someone in."

That wouldn't work for Cord. He didn't have a heart to leave open.

Chapter Five

Haley was halfway through her Saturday morning, cleaning out another stall in the old barn so any repairs needed could be easily spotted, when she heard a truck pull up. Cord. Had to be. And damn her stupid pulse for leaping at the thought.

He kissed her stupid, knocked down her defenses, and just when she was ready to let him in, he walked out. Avoided her ever since. During that time, she had the opportunity to think straight, and it dawned on her that he probably had a girlfriend, and it had been thoughts of that girl and the date he'd left the ranch for last night that had been behind his rejection.

Technically, he never said it was a date, just told her not to include him in her dinner plans and that he wouldn't be back until the next morning.

Which was now. And he was. Back.

Dammit. Already she was suffering brain farts.

He sauntered in, looking too damn sexy for her own good. Stubble on his chin, hair somewhat messed, as if he'd run his fingers through it. Gray T-shirt stretched tight over a chest she was never going to get out of her head ever again. Jeans with worn creases in all the right places, and a neutral gaze. He gave nothing away. As usual.

"Hi, Haley."

"Hey." She nodded. "So you're talking to me today?"

His lips twitched. "I deserved that. Sorry."

Surprise washed through her. Now she was curious. She headed toward him, removing her work gloves as she walked. "You feeling okay, Warlock?"

"Fine. Why?"

"It's just that 'sorry' isn't a word you say often."

"I do when it's necessary, and the way I've treated you since we kissed is unacceptable."

Holy shit. He was actually acknowledging their kiss? Her heart rocked against her ribs. Now that he had, she had absolutely no idea how to respond.

"It was a mistake. There was no reason to take it out on you," he said.

Haley stilled to the point of not breathing. A surprise? Yes. A shock? Sure. Not a mistake.

"So…are we okay?" The anxiety clouding his gaze and the tightness stiffening his broad shoulders told her that her opinion actually mattered to him.

Although they were far from okay, she nodded and smiled, determined to put his mind at ease. "Of course. We're friends," she replied, and realized it was true. "We may have come by it a little unconventionally, but I consider you a friend, nonetheless."

He nodded, letting out a breath that eased the stiffness away and his gaze cleared. "How's your arm? Do I need to change the dressing?"

"It's good," she rushed to say. Lordy, she did not need that man's hands on her. "I've been changing it."

He glanced past her and frowned. "You've been busy. I

hope you haven't overdone it. Maybe I should take a look anyway."

"I'm fine." She stepped back, because his gaze was sporting a determined gleam too strong to ignore. "And I only cleaned out two stalls. Two out of twelve is not a lot."

"It is if your arm, wrist, and hand are injured." This time he moved too quickly for her to anticipate and had her arm in his vice-like grip, examining her wound with a surprisingly gentle touch.

All the protests died on her lips and she called herself all sorts of fools. How could he render her speechless with the briefest brush of his thumb? And it wasn't even sexual. His touch was impersonal and yet, her heart was thundering in her chest, pounding away her breath.

Unreal.

She was an idiot, and proved it a few seconds later when he moved his attention to her wrist, running his thumb back and forth, causing her pulse to leap again, only this time he literally felt it.

He stilled, just like he had in her bathroom. And she remembered what had happened next. That incredible kiss. His gaze lifted to hers, all dark and smoldering, as if he, too, was reliving their kiss. Drinking and tasting like they'd been starved.

Was it bad that she wanted to taste him again?

It is if he has a girlfriend, her mind insisted. And slammed her back to reality. She was never going through that again.

Dammit.

What the hell was she doing?

Disgust washed through her body like a bucket of ice water, cooling every bit of her desire. She tugged free and stepped back. "I should get back to work," she muttered, grabbing her gloves off the ground.

He nodded, looking as bewildered as she felt. "I'll take

my things into the house then give you a hand."

No avoiding her this time?

That was a surprise. She was still contemplating that when he returned and started on the next stall.

"Stone and Brick are coming out next weekend to lend a hand," he stated. "And the following weekend, too."

She straightened and let out a breath, unaware her chest had been weighted down until some of it dissipated with his words. "That's so sweet of them. I appreciate it." She moved to the opening in the stall to glance across the way, to where he stood gripping a pitchfork, muscles flexing in his forearm, mouth grim.

He nodded. "They would've come this weekend but have a job to finish."

"Of course. I appreciate any time you all can give, as long as it doesn't interfere with Foxtrot. Or your personal life." She decided to venture. "I hope your girlfriend doesn't mind you staying here." Or the fact we can't seem to keep our hands — and lips — off each other.

His head jerked back and he frowned. "Girlfriend? I don't have a girlfriend. Jesus, you think I'd kiss you if I had a girlfriend?"

"I…" She blinked, trying to ignore the elation flowing through her from that knowledge. "It wasn't a pleasant thought. But you'd made it seem as if you'd had some sort of prearranged date last night, from the way you mentioned it the other day."

Dawning cleared the disgust from his gaze. "I did. Group therapy at At-Ease," he replied, shocking the hell out of her for two reasons.

First, because she hadn't known they started that at the ranch. And second, because never in a million years would she have pegged the tight-lipped Warlock as someone who would open up at any kind of therapy, let alone a shared one.

Her heart warmed a little further for the man who wasn't afraid to seek help if he needed it.

She cleared her throat. "Oh. I didn't know you had group therapy there. Is it new?" she asked as nonchalant as possible, needing to completely avoid the fact he was unattached.

He shrugged. "Leo suggested it a few months back after having met with the therapist in private a few times, and since it appeared to be helping him, we felt it might help a few of the other vets at the ranch."

"And has it?"

He nodded. "I think so. Each week a few more wander in."

She wanted to ask if he opened up, but that was way too personal a question and none of her business, so she nodded and changed the subject, determined to get a grin out of him. "There's something I've got to know."

His gaze turned weary. "What?"

"You any good at killing spiders? Because there's a web in the corner of the stall you're at. That's why I skipped it."

His lips twitched. "You mean the invincible Haley has a weakness?"

Bad judgment where men were concerned topped the list.

"First of all, no one is invincible. And second…hell yeah I have weaknesses." And it wasn't just spiders. She had the sinking feeling the gorgeous former Ranger regarding her with a slight gleam in his eyes was capable of wreaking havoc in her life if she let him.

So don't let him.

That gleam turned into a flicker of admiration, and that was a little more than she could handle, so she nodded and turned around to get back to work. Their attraction was palpable. Whenever they were near each other, the air around them seemed to change to a weird, heated fog. At least it had for her. Just because she became aware of every inch of sexy guy didn't mean she affected him the same way, and that really scared her. God, she hated the self-doubt. But what scared her the most was how much she enjoyed their connection. Wanted it. Craved it.

Craved *him*.

She inhaled a shaky breath. Yeah, she had weaknesses. None more dangerous than Cord. *He* topped the damn list now.

Hell, he *was* the list.

...

At the dinner table the next night, Cord did his best to be polite and contribute to the conversation, in an attempt to make up for running out on the two dinners she'd made that week. The first was an oversight. The second was his survival instinct kicking in. His inner safety mechanism after nearly combusting from that hot-as-hell kiss in her bathroom. There was no way he'd be able to sit at a table with her and pretend it never happened. Pretend he didn't want to have her for dinner, and then again for dessert.

Because, son-of-a-bitch, that was exactly what he wanted to do then…and now. He was living dangerously just being in the same room with her. She was trouble.

He was having the hardest time concentrating on what she was saying as he watched her sweet lips move, remembering how they'd tasted. Remembering how damned incredible they'd felt devouring him.

Shit.

That wasn't helping him. He ripped his gaze from her mouth, stared down at his plate, and frowned. Jesus, it was empty and he barely remembered eating the bacon cheeseburger she'd grilled while he'd taken a quick shower.

Get a damn grip, man.

Her ability to knock him off balance, to obliterate his control was a huge issue. It had to stop. He couldn't...*wouldn't* give in to his attraction to her. She was Drew's widow for Christ's sake.

His stomach knotted. How could his buddy have been so damn foolish?

Haley had been a loyal, trustworthy wife to Drew. She'd supported her husband. Never would've betrayed him or given him cause to worry, especially during deployment. He'd been so damn envious of their relationship. Why the hell had his friend jeopardized it?

You could have it now, his mind insisted.

But he wasn't looking for a woman. Didn't want that complication. Hell, he was still dealing with issues from that last mission. If he'd done his job better. If he'd been...*more*... then he wouldn't be sitting at this table now. Drew would be here helping his wife, not Cord.

Didn't matter now. That was all in the past. He was there to fulfill his promise to Drew to take care of Haley. Only, it wasn't just for Drew, was it? No. It was for himself, too. He liked Haley. There, he admitted it. He liked her. She was a good woman, and he wanted to help her out.

Even if she was stubborn as hell.

That afternoon he'd told her she could let the stall go and work in the new barn, setting up the stalls there, away from the muck, and the spiders, and heavy lifting. She'd hit him with a surly brown gaze that had as much as said, "Like hell, pal." No way was she going to leave before finishing the one she'd started.

Admiration seeped into his chest and straightened his spine. Typical Haley. Responsible. Hard headed. Beautiful.

He stilled. Not the path his thoughts needed to head.

"So, how many vets are at your ranch now?"

A safe subject. One he liked to talk about.

He lifted his gaze, finding hers filled with genuine interest. "Twenty-three," he replied. "Nineteen men, four women."

"Women?" Her brows rose. "Where do they all stay?"

"In separate barracks."

"Barracks? That's pretty great." She smiled. "So is what you do for them."

The approval in her gaze sent a responding warmth through his chest. He nodded, reaching for his water to alleviate his suddenly dry throat.

"I'm sorry I haven't gotten up there to see it." Color rose high on her cheeks, amplifying the impact of the honesty in her gorgeous brown eyes. "I feel bad. I hope you all know I think it's an incredible thing you're doing."

What was incredible was the way she regarded him with a rare genuineness that reached to his soul and soaked in like rain in a desert. If he allowed it, if he let her in, she could easily become addicting.

She already was, his mind whispered.

He ignored it.

"Thanks." He cleared his throat and fought for the control he felt slipping away at a rapid pace.

"Well, I…uh…should clear these dishes and go grab my shower." Her gaze was hesitant, and heaven help him… heated.

"I'll take care of the dishes," he offered. "You go ahead."

He needed her to leave. Now. Before he cleared the table with a quick brush of his arm to make room for her body.

Damn. What happened to her being off-limits? To not wanting complications?

They seemed to fly out the damn window with one bat of her genuine, honest eyes.

"Okay. If you're sure." She rose to her feet, hesitating while she waited for his response.

At that moment, the only thing he was sure of was if she

didn't leave, right then, he wasn't going to be able to hold onto his dwindling control. His attraction to the woman had never been stronger.

He nodded. "Yep." And to prove it, he stood and started to gather their dishes, needing to fill his hands with something to prevent him from reaching for her.

"Thanks." She smiled. "I'll only be a few minutes."

He carried his armful to the sink, grateful for the distance. "No rush," he called over his shoulder, and spent the next ten minutes returning the kitchen back to pre-dinner condition.

It was good to have a purpose. He thrived under those situations, otherwise his mind wandered. But even with a task to do, he still couldn't completely concentrate with the sound of the shower running just down the hall. His mind kept conjuring up images of Haley soaping up her lush curves, and he now sported the biggest damn hard-on he'd had in years. If not ever.

Before she finished, he needed to get to his bedroom and stay there. At least until she was safely in hers and the temptation was gone.

And just as he neared his door, the one across from it opened and Haley emerged, in a pale blue robe that clearly outlined her mouthwatering nakedness underneath.

Son-of-a-bitch.

He should've gone to the damn barn.

"Oh." She blinked and seemed to have trouble drawing in air.

Like him. Where the hell had all the air gone?

It messed with his head. Hell, his whole damn thought process ceased until his needs became wants and his wants became needs.

"You shouldn't look at me like that, Cord."

He watched, mesmerized by the pulse at the base of her neck, pounding out a crazy beat. "Like what?"

Her chest rose on a strangled inhale. "Like you want me as bad as I want you."

Ah hell. Her words energized the heat flowing through his veins, and when he lifted his gaze and found hers dark with the same fierce need racing through his body, it was too much.

It was too damn fucking much.

"Jesus, Haley, don't say stuff like that."

"Even though it's true?"

"Yes. No…fuck." He sucked in a breath, but the oxygen arrived to his brain too late.

He had already stepped into her.

Chapter Six

Sandwiched between the wall and Cord's hot, hard body—a body she'd fantasized about for years—Haley barely dared to breathe or blink in case it was just a dream.

He thrust one hand into her hair while the other palmed the wall near her head. "This is a bad idea." Those gorgeous green eyes of his were dark with hunger as he lowered his mouth to her jaw and began to kiss a slow, tantalizing path to her ear. "You need to stop me, Haley."

She knew he was right. What if he found her lacking? God, she'd never survive that. Or what if he sensed her self-doubt and she blurted out the truth about Drew? This was risky. So damn risky. She didn't want to ruin Cord's memory of his friend or have the other Rangers find out.

And yet, she didn't push him away. Instead, she clutched at his shoulders as her eyes crossed from the sheer ecstasy of his kisses. God, he made her feel desirable and wanted, and she needed that, needed that so bad right now. Maybe she could have this one time. To let his desire for her fill a little bit of the empty well where her self-confidence once resided.

She wanted him, and dammit, why shouldn't she have him this once? "How could something that feels this good be a bad idea?"

He stilled and slowly drew back to meet her gaze. "You were married to Drew."

And he'd betrayed her countless times. She owed herself this instance of pleasure. Deserved a short respite of enjoyment. She didn't owe his memory anything. "Not anymore."

Something unreadable flickered through his eyes, then disappeared before he brushed the hair off her temple. "I'm not staying. My life is in Joyful."

The honesty and concern in his gaze touched the battered and broken pieces of her heart. Warmth spread through her chest. "I know." She slid her hands to his shoulders, and butterflies fluttered low in her belly at the feel of solid muscle under her palms. "That's perfect."

"It is?"

"Yes. I'm not asking you to stay. I don't want a relationship. Been there. Done that. Lord knows I have the scars. I can't go down that road again. So don't worry, I'm not looking to connect emotionally. Just physically." She dug deep for some bravado, cupped his jaw, and caressed his delectable lower lip with her thumb. "Think you can handle that?"

When he opened his mouth to reply, she pulled him close and kissed him.

Putting all her pent up hunger, frustration, and need into it, Haley kissed him as if there were no tomorrow. Because, well, there probably wasn't. She wasn't a fool. If she managed to break through Cord's iron-tight control right now, she knew it would return by morning.

After a few incredible moments of reacquainting herself with his taste, she drew back panting.

"Haley—"

"It's okay. I know what I'm doing," she stated, unbuttoning his shirt, barely refraining from licking her lips at the expanse of tanned muscles her fingers exposed.

"You do?"

"Yeah… You."

She hoped. God, did she hope.

A night of passion hadn't been on her radar in years. It was now. And Cord was the perfect man to deliver. A spark simmered under the surface with them. He made her burn. And since it wasn't permanent and their hearts weren't involved, when he left her ranch and returned to At-Ease, she'd watch him walk away with a smile on her face, and God willing, some much needed confidence.

Cord remained silent, but arousal flared in his eyes, and darkened with resolution and something else. He shrugged out of the shirt she'd unbuttoned then reached for the tie on her robe. "Be sure about this."

She grasped his wrist and helped him tug her robe open. "I'm sure if you don't quit talking and get started, I'm going to give the honor to my plastic friend in my nightstand."

"Hell no. Not while I'm around." He jerked the tie the rest of the way, and when it came loose, her robe parted, and his eyes darkened to a deep emerald as he looked his fill. "Damn, Haley."

His words and tone matched the appreciation in his eyes, and her barbeque potato chip fetish suddenly didn't seem like such a bad indulgence. Empowered by his hungry expression, she reached for the band of his jeans, but he grasped her wrist and pulled it away.

"Not yet. It's time to take care of you."

Her?

Some of her surprise must've shown on her face, because he lifted a brow. She knew what he wanted to ask: *Drew didn't take care of you first?*

She lifted a shoulder, and that was all the response he was going to get out of her. She was done bringing her late husband into their...whatever this was going on between them.

Unable to resist the magnificence in front of her, Haley trailed her hands over his broad, naked expanse of chest, scraping her nails over his nipples on her journey south. He hissed a breath and captured her wrists in one swift move that had him holding them above her head as he pressed her against the wall with all that muscle.

"You first, remember?" His breath was hot, his gaze was dark and intense, and his body...oh God...his body slid down then up, and the delicious feel of his hot, hard flesh against hers ripped a moan from her throat.

It was that good. And she wanted more. Needed more.

Ever the intuitive, he wedged his thigh between hers, and slid again. And yet again, all the while staring deep into her eyes, as if gauging her reactions. The unexpected friction against her sensitive flesh had her crying out and his eyes dilating.

"Like that?" he asked in a rough voice that told her he was getting just as much pleasure from the sweet torture.

She opened her mouth to respond, but nothing came out, because he simply stole her breath. So she nodded and rocked into him, needing to let him know he felt so damn good.

"I want you, Haley." He transferred her wrists to one hand and skimmed the other slowly down her body, causing a slew of new sensations to race to her toes. "Have for some time."

That knowledge did crazy, wonderful things to her battered ego. The ever-present, crushing weight of her inadequacies lightened and her pulse jumped in her veins.

"Me, too," she managed on a whisper.

"I don't usually give in to my wants," he murmured,

dipping down to brush his mouth to her throat. "I concentrate on my needs. But you're on both sides of that coin."

Lord knew he was on both sides of her coin. And making her hot. God, so hot.

His mouth was blazing a trail to her jaw now, and her fingers curled in her trapped hands, waiting as anticipation rocked her heart against her ribs.

"Last chance to stop." He held her gaze, as they shared a breath.

"Okay," she replied, her lips brushing his as she spoke. She was all for stopping his teasing.

With a groan rumbling in his chest, he finally took her lips for the kiss she'd burned for all evening. Hot and demanding, over and over, he devoured her strength, and she trembled against him. His hand was stroking high on her ribs, the very tips of his fingers brushing the bottom of her breast.

She moaned and arched into his touch, encouraging more. Much more. He released her wrists to cup both breasts, brushing her nipples back and forth with his thumbs. Yes... that. Her arms were tingling as she lowered them to run her hands on him everywhere. His muscled chest and broad back, around his lean sides to explore the ridges of his abs that quivered under her touch.

He was magnificent.

When he released her mouth, he stepped back to slide her robe off her shoulders and watched as the material landed at her feet. Then his gaze made a slow, burning trail all the way up to her eyes. His were hot. Hungry. Intense.

"God, Haley," he murmured, gruff and so damn sexy she didn't know what to do with herself. "Turn around."

Wanting nothing more than to keep that look, that level of craving in him, alive, she did, pushing back that damn self-doubt. There was no room for it under the heat of his desire.

He groaned and trailed a finger down her spine until he

cupped her ass with both hands. "So gorgeous."

The sexy man was both feeding her ego and seriously taxing her strength at the same time. Need raced through her body, pooling at all her good parts, and she shook from the power of it. "Cord…"

"Right here," he muttered, pulling her with him until they were in the bathroom, standing in front of the vanity and large mirror above. "Look how gorgeous you are."

She saw him. Only him, and the muscles in the arm banding her middle, the big hand covering her breast, and those eyes… God, those gorgeous green eyes of his smoldered as he watched his hand trail down her body to disappear between her legs.

Breath hitched in her chest and desire burst out as he sank his teeth into the curve of her neck at the same instant his thick finger slid home. She whimpered and pressed back, rubbing against the large bulge in his jeans. "Please."

"Christ." His mouth was at her nape, making her shiver. "Anything you want."

With a rough sound vibrating through his chest and into her back, he nipped at her shoulder and caught her nipple between his thumb and forefinger, all while grinding his erection into her bottom. It was too much, and so damn good. Sensations ricocheted through her body, declaring the man gifted beyond reason. Lost in pleasure she suddenly worried only Cord could bring, her eyes drifted shut and her head fell back to rest on his shoulder.

"Just you," she finally replied in a pant as she gripped his hips and rocked with the rhythm of his hand. More tremors raced down her legs and her knees wobbled. "I can't stand."

He shoved that wonderful thigh between hers again and steadied her while he continued to ravage her body. "I've got you. Just relax."

She did, and opened wider at his urging, moaning when

he changed the angle and upped the pace. "Oh...I..." She tightened the grip on his hips and bucked. "Harder," she urged, so very close to that blissful edge his touch promised.

"Come for me, Haley." He stroked her harder, longer, and when he added his thumb to the mix, brushing her center with the right amount of pressure, she burst, going off like a bottle rocket from all the pent up need the man caused the past few days.

When the room finally came into focus and he brought her down slow and easy, she watched his finger pull out and satisfaction gleam in his eyes. "You're so wet."

"Your fault." She grinned at his reflection then squeaked when he quickly turned her to face him.

"Damn right," he growled, his mouth coming down on hers for a hot, demanding, possessive kiss as he lifted her into his arms and carried her across the hall and into his room.

Without breaking their kiss, he set her on the mattress, his tongue brushing hers in an erotic dance she longed to mimic with the rest of their bodies. She slid her hands up his chest, throat, over his scruffy jaw, yearning to feel the roughness on her skin. It was arousing and intimate. And when he drew back, his eyes were heated and unwavering. He made her feel fierce, protected, and beautiful.

God, how was it he could make her feel so much with just a glance?

He was incredible, and had always been popular with the ladies. What if she didn't measure up?

She cleared her throat. "It's been a long time for me."

Not the best time to get shy. But the last thing she wanted was to disappoint the man. God, she just couldn't bear that.

"Haley."

She skimmed her hands down to his jeans, brushing her fingers along the band, in love with the feel of the taut skin of his rigid, hard washboard abs vibrating under her touch.

Her own insides quivered in response.

"Haley," he repeated, and thrust his fingers into her hair, holding her head as his gaze bored deep. "You could never disappoint me."

"How…?" She just blinked up at Cord. "I didn't say—"

A smile tugged his lips. "Your body told me," he replied, his words hot along her skin as his lips grazed her jaw.

"Yeah?" Damn mind reader. Or body reader, apparently. "What is it telling you now?"

She popped the buttons on his jeans before slipping her fingers inside to free him. Sweet mercy, he was hard and big and pulsing in her hand.

His jaw clenched. "*Fuck*."

"Right again."

He choked out a laugh and she grinned, but her amusement died on her lips when he started to shuck the rest of his clothes. She pushed up onto her elbows and eagerly watched The Cord Show. He wasn't as tall as Drew, but he sported more ridges, and muscles, and…length.

Magnificent. She couldn't get enough air into her lungs to elaborate. "You're beautiful," she managed.

He dug a condom from his pocket, then dropped the jeans to tear open the packet. "The only one beautiful here is you." Always the great multi-tasker, he rolled on the condom while striding to the bed. When he gently grasped her ankles and spread her legs apart, her breath caught again. He gazed at her. "See? Absolutely gorgeous."

Chapter Seven

Cord knew they'd crossed a big line, but desire had gotten the better of him. Wore him down. All damn weekend, he'd rehashed his conversation with the guys. *Drew gave his blessing.* Leo's words echoed through his head, making him wonder if maybe they were right. But it was Haley's acquiescence—her admittance she wanted him—that finally did him in. He'd wanted her, too. For so fucking long. No way could he resist what she'd offered.

He crawled up her sexy-as-hell body, addicted to pressing his lips to her skin, loving how soft and supple she felt underneath him. She was so damn beautiful, and still trying to catch her breath. He smiled against her curves. Knowing he could bring her to that state felt incredible, and he wanted to do it over and over again.

Capturing a delectable nipple between his lips, he pressed it between his tongue and the roof of his mouth. A helpless, needy sound rumbled through her chest, and she ground her hips against him. Heat funneled south in a swift rush, throbbing through his dick. It blew his mind how her hunger matched his own.

He pulled back and blew on her nipple, watching a shiver wrack her body. She *still* couldn't catch her breath. Good.

Intent on keeping her in that state, he kissed a path up to her mouth and changed the pace, brushing first one side of her full lips, then the other, before settling right on. The soft sweep of her tongue against his sent a jolt straight to his groin. Shy or bold, the woman turned him on big time. He wanted, needed, *craved* both sides of her.

Her whole body was trembling underneath him now, and he didn't remember ever feeling so…lucky. So damn lucky. The urge to elicit more reactions had him releasing her mouth to explore the soft spot behind her ear again.

She moaned and squirmed and turned her head to offer him more. Three responses. He was on a roll. Never a slacker, he took advantage of the opportunity and kissed a path to the curve of her neck where he sank his teeth into her flesh, then soothed the sting with his tongue, remembering how she'd loved it in the bathroom.

"Cord," she breathed, clutching his back.

He repeated the process while he snuck a hand between their bodies to brush over her folds before he slipped a finger inside. Her moan mingled with his.

"So wet." He needed to be insider her. Needed to have her.

She rocked into him, encouraging him to give her what she needed. "Cord…please…"

Hell, she didn't need to beg. He was more than ready.

Positioning himself at her opening, he groaned. Damn, he'd never felt anything so exquisite. Then she arched, trying to take what she wanted, but he held her firmly in place, his fingers digging into her hips. He needed to slow her down.

"More," she demanded.

"Don't want to hurt you."

"You'll hurt me only if you don't move."

He chuckled, but it strangled in his throat at the feel of her wrapping her legs around his ass, forcing him to slide into her sweetness.

"Christ, Haley, you feel so damn good." Too perfect to keep the feeling inside.

Apparently she agreed, because she echoed with a long, low moan. "Finally your turn?"

Didn't she get it? Didn't she understand what she did to him?

"Been my turn all along."

Every stroke. Every kiss. Every damn one of her sighs had him so hard and throbbing he was ready to burst. But he needed to take this slow, to savor this gift. Commit it to memory.

She rocked her hips. Fuck, that felt good, and her low, throaty moan that followed was like a physical stroke to his dick. His need to drive in and out of her trumped his need to take it slow. He began to move, finding the right rhythm that melted his spine.

"Damn…that's good," she murmured, bucking beneath him, driving him bat-shit crazy.

He leaned down to claim her lips in a hot, wild, demanding kiss, dipping his tongue inside her mouth to mimic their thrusting bodies. So incredible. He pulled nearly all the way out, then drove home, harder, faster—deeper—loving how she clutched at his arms and sighed his name. God, he loved the sound of his name on her lips. It was insane. Addicting. Fucking perfect. Hovering on the edge, he rejoiced in the combination of torment and ecstasy. It was a ride unlike any he'd ever experienced before.

"Cord…"

"I know."

Reaching under her sweet ass, he spread her just enough

to sink in a little farther and the new angle had him filling her to the hilt. So damn good. He knew it would be this good. On an inhale, she arched back and moaned, brushing her gorgeous breasts and tight nipples against his chest. That was it. He was done. She decimated his control.

"Open your eyes, Haley." His voice sounded rough. He was barely hanging on. "Open your eyes and come with me."

Her eyelids fluttered open, and she locked onto his gaze, hers dark and full of need. He wasn't alone. She was just as lost in this craziness. And as he drew back then pushed all the way inside, he watched her burst with his name on her sweet lips.

It was his undoing.

"Christ, Haley." He thrust hard within her, lost in the feel of her gripping him tight, lost in *her,* and that was where he found his own long, fierce release.

Coming down from the high, he kissed her through the aftermath, in frantic, deep passes. Then he changed the tempo, and softly brushed his mouth to hers, before moving up to kiss her forehead.

They stayed that way for several moments while working to catch their breath. He couldn't have moved if he needed to. The incredible woman stole his bones and, he suspected, much more.

• • •

"That was much better than I remember," Haley admitted, body still trembling. She knew with their chemistry it would be incredible, but this was far surpassing her expectations. And gauging the reactions she saw and felt in him, Cord enjoyed it, too.

"Yeah?" He lifted up to gaze down at her. "Much better than your plastic friend?"

A smile tugged at her lips. "Yeah." She lifted a hand to scrape her knuckles over his jaw. "Hell yeah."

"I like 'hell yeah.'" Then he did something she didn't see often enough—he smiled, a genuine smile that reach his eyes and softened the hard lines of his face. It was like the sun breaking over the horizon. Breathtaking.

She traced his lower lip. "I like it, too."

He bent down to kiss her quick then rolled off the bed and vanished into the bathroom.

When he came back out, and she watched his fine ass stride to his discarded clothes instead of her, she lifted up on her elbow and raised a brow. "Where's the fire?"

Jeans in hand, he straightened and glanced over at her, and her sensitized body reacted as if he caressed her with his hands. "Thought this was a one-time thing."

With his short hair tussled, thanks to her fingers, heat still lingering in his gaze, and the fact he was still semi-hard, he looked dangerous and delicious, and her "one-time thing" bit the dust.

"It was more of one night type thing, and there's plenty of night left." She patted the mattress, hope and anticipation fluttering in her chest.

His gaze slid slowly over her again. A second later his jeans hit the floor, but not before he withdrew another condom, which he slapped on the nightstand then turned to stare down at her. "You sure?" he asked, voice deliciously gruff.

"Yes." She reached out to take him gently in her hands and stroke. "Very. Unless you don't have the stamina," she teased, knowing it was far from true.

"I've got it as long as you need it." He thrust into her hand, growing deliciously harder with each stroke.

Her heart rocked against her ribs and sent a surge of heat through her body. "Even if I need it all night?"

With a slight smile reaching his eyes again, he climb in on top of her, and his body relaxed deliciously into hers. She wasn't sure she'd ever felt anything so erotic.

Sprawled over her, he entwined their fingers and lifted their joined hands to either side of her face. "I'm at my best at night."

And he proved it.

Chapter Eight

Cord woke up to an empty bed. Normally, that would be great, but for some reason it messed with his head. Haley had rocked his world several times last night…until he'd run out of condoms. Then this morning, she'd walked out before dawn.

Usually his role. It was weird to have it reversed on him.

And by Haley, of all women…

He shook his head and lay there staring at the ceiling, replaying the incredible night. Soft, and willing, and hungry. She had satisfied him like no other. Being inside her, watching her fly apart was so damn addicting. Her reactions to his touch, the fact she knew exactly how and where to stroke, and the way her rhythm had matched his own blew his fucking mind. He'd always known they'd be good in bed. How could they not with that ever-present attraction simmering between them? Christ, she could own him. So damn easily.

If he let her.

For the better part of Cord's life, he forced himself to keep every emotion in check. He had a mother, grandmother, and kid sister to take care of and protect. Then soldiers and civilians.

It was ingrained in him. He kept everything in check. Played it close to the vest. So watching her take pleasure in him and in pleasing him, he found it mesmerizing. *She* was mesmerizing. Intoxicating, and he hadn't been able to get enough of her, not her sighs, her taste, the feel of her soft curves writhing beneath him, or her tiny little pants when he was buried deep inside her sweet heat… *Fuck*. He was hard again. Or was that still? With Haley, it was beginning to blur.

Damn, he didn't need that added complication.

After grabbing a quick shower, he made his way to the kitchen, not sure what to expect. Now that he was wide awake and free of his Haley-induced sexual stupor, he saw things clearer. It hadn't been smart to bring sex into the mix. What the hell had he done?

You had sex with Drew's widow, his mind supplied, and shards of guilt hollowed his gut.

Fuck.

What if Haley was feeling guilty, too?

It was all on him. His fault. He should've been stronger. Stood his ground. Kept his damn hands off her. Instead of helping out, he was only adding to the poor woman's troubles. Christ. He still had two weeks left at the ranch, and in one night, he might've screwed the whole thing up.

A second later, he walked into the kitchen, ready to face the music, only to find it empty except for a dirty mug and dish in the sink. He glanced out the window, not surprised to find Haley's silhouette in one of the far corrals. Up at dawn as usual. Why should today be any different? Just because he could still barely find his bones didn't mean she had that problem.

That was good. Right?

It sure as shit didn't feel good.

Cord caught himself scowling and blew out a breath.

Putting aside the Drew issue, he evaluated his uncharacteristic attitude. The woman wanted one night of sex and, hell, that's all he'd wanted, too. But now that she was going on with business as usual, he was, what... Pouting? Christ, he should be *grateful*. It was every guy's dream to have hot, wild sex without the aftermath of clingy.

So why the hell did he feel awful?

Because he was a fucking idiot, that's why.

As if to confirm that, his phone started to ring with Brick on the line.

"How goes things in Haley land?"

Cord's whole body tightened with the images those words provoked. He knew exactly how Haley land looked...and felt.

In-fucking-credible.

He cleared his throat. "Fine. What's got you calling so early?"

"Stone's doing a follow-up with McGregor today and he wanted to know where you put the last of the invoices."

He shook his head to clear it. "In the invoice box on the desk." Exactly where they belonged.

Brick's chuckle echoed through the phone. "Jovy has the office so clean and organized he can't find a damn thing."

"Apparently." Cord flicked the phone on speaker and set it on the counter so he could fish out a slice of bread and drop it in the toaster.

He would've been happy to drop some in for Haley, too, except, *oh...that's right*, she already ate and started work without him.

Christ, he needed to stop acting so butt-hurt. They had their agreed upon one night. Hell, he didn't want any more than that, either. So why wasn't he smiling and walking lighter, like a guy who'd had fantastic sex with a hot chick?

Because she'd turned the tables on him. Did what he'd done to women his whole life. She'd given and taken what she'd wanted from him and left before dawn to avoid the awkward morning after…and he was belly-aching about it? "I need my head examined."

"I could've told you that." Brick's second chuckle filled the air. "But just out of curiosity, what made you come to that conclusion?"

"Forget it."

"Oh…ho…no, buddy. You and Haley have this crazy-ass chemistry thing going on. We already established Drew had given his blessing, and now you're there alone with her for another two weeks, and you expect me to forget it? Forget that. What's going on?"

Cord hung up and shoved his phone back in his pocket.

Another two weeks with Haley. An unrecognizable emotion rippled through his gut as he finished his toast and gulped down a cup of coffee. No room in his life for unrecognizable emotions, so he labeled it akin to lust and straightened his shoulders. He'd manage.

After cleaning up his mess, he grabbed his hat off the chair, where he'd set it the night before, and headed outside to start his day. He had the second half of the roof to patch up before the sun got too high in the sky and broiled him for lunch.

But on his way to the barn, he noticed Haley stopped pounding on a post and lifted a hand to wave at him. Apparently he still existed to her. Good to know. He just wished he knew whether to nod and keep going, or was he supposed to change direction and head to her for some kind of after sex talk.

Shit.

This was all his damn fault.

His insides clenched. Why the hell did he have to go complicate things with sex?

Considering how long she'd ruled his fantasies, and how

much hotter reality turned out to be, those complications blurred. And as he watched her walk toward him in pair of cutoffs and hard-on inducing work boots, a fitted T-shirt with the words NEED CHOCOLATE printed across her chest—the material the same warm brown as her eyes—she rendered him brainless.

"Morning, beautiful," he murmured before his mouth could reconnect to his brain.

Oh, that's right, he didn't have one at the moment. She sucked it from his soul, with those mile-long legs of hers, and the lazy, warm smile of a woman who'd been satisfied many times the night before.

By him. He'd put that look on her pretty face, and if that didn't make him feel ten feet tall, nothing would.

She stopped in front of him and her smile increased. "It *is* a good morning, thanks to you."

The uptight, serious version of Haley was nowhere in sight. He liked both, but maybe this one a little more. The morning breeze lifted the hair off her temple, and his fingers itched to catch the strand he knew to feel silky and soft.

Jesus, what the hell was he doing getting urges like that?

"About last night," he started, and then cleared his throat. Morning afters were never trouble for him. What the hell? He suddenly didn't know what to say. But this was Haley. He couldn't just brush her off. Besides, she was smiling an actual smile—at him. It was sweet and glowing…and sweet.

Damn.

It didn't help that she was the most beautiful thing he'd ever seen. Always had been. Still. He wasn't looking for anything, and neither was she. And then there was the fucking whopper—she was Drew's wife. At least, she had been. So, he needed to find his damn tongue, and fast. "Do we need to talk about last night?"

"I don't know. Do we?"

He narrowed his gaze, at a complete loss for words.

"It's okay, Cord," she said in a soft tone. "We can talk about it if you need to."

"Me?" He reeled back, baffled. "I thought that's why you came over."

She chuckled softly and set her palms on his chest. "Nope. I wanted this."

Before his vacant head registered her words, she lifted up on tiptoe and took what she wanted in a long, thorough, hungry kiss that rendered them both breathless. It wasn't just a brain missing from his head. Lack of blood in his noggin made him dizzy. Luckily, there was enough sense left for a flicker of concern to register.

Jesus, he hoped she remembered he wasn't staying. That he was just temporary, because that wasn't what he was getting from her kiss. "Haley—" he began when they drew apart, but she cut him off.

"Relax, Cord." She patted his arm like a child who needed comforting.

Christ, he wasn't a kid. Hell, he didn't even remember being one. And he certainly didn't feel like one when she had her mouth on him. Like now.

Her lips grazed his jaw. "I was looking for fun and temporary. So don't sweat it, *Warlock*. Your bachelorhood is not in jeopardy." She drew back and patted his chest. "You're safe. And don't even think about bringing Drew into this. He's part of the past. What happened was between you and me. Is it too much to ask for you to just let me enjoy the memory of an amazing night?"

He released a breath and the little pinpricks of tension eased from his shoulders. She wasn't harboring guilt. He hadn't added to her troubles. In fact, going by the warm, lazy smile on her face, he'd say she was feeling pretty good at the moment. And it was his fault. "*You* are something else, Haley."

"I think you liked that something else last night." Her grin was teasing and carefree and it pulled one from him with such ease it should've alarmed him.

It probably would have if he'd had even a quarter of brain matter left in his head, and if she hadn't been right. But she *was* right. Last night, he'd thought her a lot of things, not the least of which was amazing as hell, and a damn sight better than his fantasies.

"I'll let you in on a little secret." She leaned in close enough he could smell her perfume. It was light and citrusy…a contradiction, like the woman. "I thought the same about you."

He blinked, trying not to feel too good about her admission, but damn, he had the strangest urge to pound his chest. "Yeah?"

"Oh yeah." She winked and sent him a sweet smile, conjuring up more contradictions — or *Haley-isms* — appearing innocent and wicked at the same time.

The boots. Had to be the damn boots, with her long expanse of supple legs teasing his sanity. Or maybe it was all of her.

"There's more to you than just a hot body," she said, regarding him closely. "Beneath all the muscles and ridges and that damn *V* that messes with my head, is a giving heart. You just don't realize it."

"You sure you're talking about me? I don't have a heart," he stated. The last thing he needed was her thinking she'd touched his heart. Maybe every other part of him, including a few of his favorite parts, but there had been no movement in his chest.

Except there so was. Damn. Like now. His heart rocked against his ribs at the sound of her laughter.

"Bullshit," she said, and her gaze twinkled as she leaned up and kissed him again. Sweet, open-mouthed kisses that turned hot when her tongue brushed his, blowing his meager gathering of brain cells out to the pasture on his left. God, she tasted good. But before he could gather her close, she whirled out of his arms and headed back to work on her fence with a smile on her face.

He stood slack-jawed, staring after the woman who just kissed the hell out of him then walked away. Like last night. His butt really needed to get over it already.

This was ideal. She didn't demand more. Didn't try to get him to take her out, or fish for compliments. Nothing.

In fact, she told him *he* was great. Reassured *him* his bachelor status was not on her radar. It was fucking perfect.

So why the hell did it feel like he'd been run over by a tank?

Chapter Nine

It was mid-morning on Wednesday and Haley was filled with an excitement she hadn't felt in years. She was heading to the high school to check out the town swap meet and support the football team and their fundraising. A win/win. But the best part was that Cord was joining her.

"I'll be ready in a few minutes," he said, walking into the house. He was going with her to scout out some supplies for the stalls. "I need to grab a quick shower first."

And she needed to wait outside, because being in the house while he was naked and wet just down the hall was way too tempting on her resolve to keep their one-time thing…a one-time thing.

She grabbed her purse, notepad, and pen, and headed outside on the porch to wait for a fully clothed Cord to emerge. Playing it smart was the way she'd have to roll while he was at the ranch. It was safer, too. Taking advantage of the time, she jotted down ideas of supplies to look for, and had just settled on one when Cord stepped onto the porch.

Her heart leaped in her chest. Being fully clothed did

nothing to lessen his sex appeal. A pair of jeans—faded in all the right places—hugged his lean hips and stole her breath. With *safe* and *smart* uppermost in her mind, she immediately ripped her gaze from the "danger zone" to take in the light gray T-shirt stretched to perfection, and the…Stetson?

Dayam. She was used to seeing either his Ranger cover or simple ball cap on his head. Catching a glimpse of his cowboy side made him appear 100 percent Texan. And she was 100 percent appreciative.

"Ready?" he asked.

Lordy, was she ever…

"Yep." Shaking off her Cord stupor, she shoved her notepad and pen into her purse and stood. "Let's go." Before the stupor returned.

By the time they pulled into the busy high school parking lot, she regained control of her mental faculties and happily answered his questions about the town and the school.

"How long did you go here?" he asked, cutting the engine.

"A year and a half," she replied. "I was halfway through my junior year when my uncle got custody of me."

His gaze narrowed on her. "Must've been tough."

She shrugged. "It got easier when I moved in with Uncle John. Bouncing back and forth between my mother's two sisters was tough. I liked being with him instead."

Cord nodded. "Upheaval is tough. Especially at a young age."

His tone bespoke of experience, and her heart lurched at the implication.

"Did you move around when you were a kid?"

"Just once," he replied. "We sold our ranch after my dad died and moved to Austin to live with my grandmother. Lizzy was ten. It was hard on her at first."

Her heart squeezed at the thought of all the younger Cord had gone through. She had no trouble envisioning him stepping up to fill his father's shoes as head of the family. Shame he hadn't learned to step back yet.

She set a hand on his arm, and he turned a startled gaze on her. "Had to be hard on you, too. How old were you? Fourteen? Fifteen?"

Something unreadable passed through his eyes. "Almost fifteen."

It explained his responsible demeanor and why he tugged free and slipped from the truck. He was uncomfortable talking about himself.

Too bad.

"You got a job after school, didn't you?" she asked, meeting him in front of the truck.

His lips twitched, but he didn't elaborate.

"I'll take that as a yes." She chuckled and fell into step alongside him on their way toward the football field full of vendors, and the sign permanently honoring Drew, Whitney High's all-American hero.

People in town still came up to her gushing about his glory days, or how he'd helped this one out at their ranch, or that one at their hardware store, telling her how lucky she had been to be his wife. And for the most part, they were right. The other part, she kept to herself. They didn't need to know Drew's shortcomings. Neither did his Ranger buddies. And they wouldn't. Not by her.

Her husband's death had to be hardest on Cord and Brick. The three had gone through training together. That was why it was important to her to make sure their memories remained fond. She could tell by the way he stiffened up after reading the sign that it was still hard for him.

"Drew never mentioned you went to school together," Cord said.

"Because we didn't. He was five years ahead of me. We met in Colorado on a rafting trip."

"Small world."

She nodded. And a cruel one at times. But she wasn't going to let it be today. No, today they were going to have a little bit of fun. "How are you at throwing ping pong balls into fishbowls?"

It was one of her favorite game stands sprinkled in throughout the flea market.

His gaze lightened and his lips twitched. "Good. I used to win them for Lizzie all the time."

"Yeah?" She raised a brow. "So am I. Care to take me on? All the proceeds for the games go to the football team."

He cocked his head. "Depends. What does the winner get? And don't say the fish."

"Darn." She chuckled. "Fine. How about the loser gets to mow the south pasture in this blazing heat?"

She watched his expression and smiled at the battle she knew was going on in his head. He already assumed she would lose and be the one to cut the pasture, but he didn't want her to do that chore. Since arriving at her ranch, he had yet to let her cut anything. The way she figured it, she was a winner either way.

"Alright." Challenge sparked in his eyes and brightened his features. "You're on."

Setting his hand at the small of her back, he guided her through the crowd to the fish booth where they settled into a spot between two families. He handed money to a teenager working the stand, and the kid set a basket of ping pong balls in front of them.

"Ladies first," Cord said, standing back to give her room.

She smiled. "Okay, but I'm only tossing six; you get the other half."

Last thing she needed was a dozen fish, which was possible if they landed all twelve balls. By the time she finished, four of her six were floating in colored water, and the only reason it hadn't been all six was because her balls had collided with others midair.

Smiling, she switched places with a smirking Cord and watched him land five out of his six. Dammit.

"Wow, you two are good." A cute little boy on her right blinked up at her and Cord, adoration rounding his big brown eyes. "I was trying to win some for my sister over there but didn't get any in the bowls." He pointed to a sweet toddler in a stroller reaching for him and saying, "Sishy."

"Well, I think we can help you out," Cord said, then met her gaze briefly before turning to the teenager manning the booth and held up two fingers.

Her heart cracked open and warmth spread through her chest at his sweet gesture. He was something else.

She cleared her throat and smiled down at the little boy. "I'm sure you would've landed two, but mine hit yours and knocked them away."

"Here you go." Cord presented the boy with two bags filled with water and a gold fish.

Those big brown eyes widened again. "Wow. Thanks! I'm gonna have my sister name them after you. What's your names?"

"Cord and Haley," she replied, her stomach fluttering at the thought of their namesakes sharing a fish bowl. Silly, she knew this, but somehow it also felt intimate.

After the little boy's parents thanked them and walked away, Cord turned to her and raised a brow. "You want the other fish we won?"

"No." She laughed. "It was mostly about the challenge."

Mischief gleamed in his emerald eyes. "You up for another one? Or are you afraid of losing again?"

Why that...

"Oh, you're going down, pal." She grabbed his hand and tugged him to the next booth.

In the back of her mind, she knew they had supplies to

buy, but it was early yet. Besides, for the first time in years, she was feeling happy and carefree, and she got the sense it had been even longer for him.

・・・

Before Cord knew it, an hour had passed and he was at the final game stand with Haley. The dart game…and she was kicking his ass. Damn darts seemed to bounce right off the balloons he hit while hers popped with ease. But that was okay. Her arms were full of the prizes he'd won. All he carried was a rolled up T-shirt from her prowess at pitching dimes on a plate.

He watched, mesmerized by the way she bit her lower lip as she concentrated on her last dart.

"Yes," she cried out triumphantly after popping her final balloon.

There was no way he could win. Not with only one dart left. He set it down and faced the grinning woman. "Great job, Haley. What do you do? Sleep with those things under your pillow?" he teased.

She laughed. "No. I did an article on Irish pubs, once, and played across Ireland for research. I'm a quick study."

"Lady's choice," the kid behind the stand said, motioning to his stash of gaudy stuffed animals.

Christ. His gut clenched. She was probably going to pick the biggest, ugliest stuffed animal. What the hell was he going to do with it?

"That one." She pointed to something but smiled at him over her shoulder, and the pure joy lighting her eyes caught and held his attention. He'd never seen anyone so genuine, so damn beautiful.

No prize could top that smile.

"Here you go." She stepped close to shove a bright neon-green plush animal into his chest. "Every Warlock needs a dragon."

He snickered and grabbed his prize, his fingers brushing over hers.

She cleared her throat. "Think he's bright enough?" she asked, her voice a little breathless.

"Hell yeah. I bet they can see him from the space station." He smirked. "Thanks for that, by the way."

Her laughter echoed between them. "You're welcome. Never let it be said I didn't take care of the great Warlock."

Thing was, she took real good care of him. No woman had ever bothered to worry about what he wanted. Haley did. It hadn't escaped his notice how his favorite things showed up at each meal. She somehow took note of his likes and dislikes and adjusted the meals to suit him. If it wasn't for the fact he knew she enjoyed what she placed on the table then he would've protested. She was something else. She even brought water to him throughout the day, right when he needed it. How the hell did she do that? How did she know? She seemed in tuned to his needs. It was the strangest thing.

And nice. Damn nice. So was the feel of her soft skin. He was reluctant to let her go, but they had too much stuff to carry. "What do you say we take this loot back to the truck before we grab lunch?"

"Sounds good."

Together they walked to his truck and dropped their winnings on the seat before heading back in search of lunch. His to-do list at the ranch wasn't getting any shorter, but he refused to rush Haley. He chanced a glance at her, noting the sweet smile still curving her lips. It'd been present most of the morning, and he was reluctant to see it end. He was playing with fire. He knew it but didn't care.

Being with her like this was nice. Tension seemed to ease from his body in her presence. He was content. Happy. He could breathe. It was nice to breathe without the usual heaviness in his chest. Where the hell it went, he had no idea. It was just gone.

She led him to a stand with the biggest crowd. "Beauregard's has the best barbeque."

Again. The amazing woman did it again. Out of all the choices for lunch, she chose the one he would've picked.

Standing at the end of the line, she turned to him and set her hand on his arm. "Thanks, Cord."

"For what?" He frowned, liking the feel of her touch more than he should.

"For today," she replied.

His lips twitched. "Beating you at the games?"

"Hey. I won two." She punched his shoulder.

"I know." Reaching out, he quickly sandwiched her hand between his palm and bicep. "I have a blinding dragon to remind me."

"Keep it up and I'll exchange it for the bright pink pig."

She would, too. Her gaze was full of mischief.

"Point taken."

"Then I hope you get my other point," she said, her expression turning serious. "I had a good time this morning. Better than I have in years. Thank you for that, Cord."

"I had a good time, too."

She nodded, hand still on his arm, apparently not in any more of a hurry than him to break their connection. "We're a pair. Maybe while you're at the ranch we should make sure we don't let each other get too serious. Kind of hold each other in check, or out of check."

If it meant seeing more of her smiles, he was all for it and quickly agreed, despite the warning bells going off in his head.

He ignored the bastards.

For most of his life he heeded them, but maybe it was time to buck his own system. To do as she suggested…get "out of check."

What harm could it do?

Chapter Ten

A few days later, Haley was working alongside Cord, still mending fences, and trying not to think about the fence she'd forged with Cord the other night. Their crazy chemistry had blazed out of control until they'd given in, and now it seemed to have forged something stronger, hotter...solid.

Even though they hadn't given in again, she couldn't get the damn man out of her head. Or their incredible night. Or the fact she wanted more. Dammit. But their deal had been for one night, and other than those extra few kisses she stole the following morning, she'd held good to her word and fell into an easy working relationship with her guest.

That was what he was. Her guest.

Not the hot hunk of a man who gave her mind-blowing orgasm after orgasm in the space of one night. Nope. That was the past. Now, he was her guest there to help out around the ranch until the end of the month.

She glanced at him from under her lashes. The lines around his mouth were less rigid. Same with his broad shoulders, which were now rippling with lean muscles under a T-shirt stretched tight across his back with each swing of the sledgehammer that drove the post home. She ripped her gaze away and inhaled as her mind wanted to go to that naughty place, but she behaved. The man was there to get the ranch in shape for her grand opening, not become her sex slave. She smiled at the thought. As if anyone could make the mighty Cord Brannigan do what he didn't want to do. That's why it made her feel good to know the ranch wasn't the only thing benefiting from his stay. Cord was improving, too.

He'd loosened up enough to crack a smile once in a while, and even converse more than a few words. And the biggie… he remained in a room with her for more than twenty minutes now. Apparently, the idiot realized she wasn't coveting a relationship with him. In fact, he kind of seemed a little put out about it, as if he wondered why she didn't.

Haley smiled. It was kind of empowering to keep such an alpha, virile guy off balance. Certainly healed some of her battered ego. She had a long way to go, but it was a start. Still, she didn't let it go to her head. If there was one thing she knew about Warlock, it was his ability to adapt to any situation. Her time with the upper hand was running out. Fast.

But that was okay. She wasn't sure she wanted to seduce him again. Why couldn't he seduce her? Why couldn't he want her as bad as she wanted him?

Misgivings began to ripple through her gut.

He did, her self-preservation side insisted, quelling her fears. It'd been written in the fierce, intense pleasure on his face when he drove in and out of her the other night, over and over, like he wanted to prolong his release, as if being buried inside her had been the most incredible feeling in the world.

It had been for her. *So* incredible.

If she closed her eyes, she could still feel the pressure of him on top of her, feel him moving inside her. See the ecstasy on his face when he thrust deep and climaxed. Her insides quivered just thinking about it.

Once hadn't been enough. God, she'd been so greedy. Her mind replayed the things she'd done to him, and things she'd let him do to her, and warmth flooded her cheeks. By rights, she should be embarrassed, and probably would be…if it hadn't felt so freaking amazing.

For years, she'd put her desires second. Her mistake. Maybe if she'd acted on them with Drew more often, he wouldn't have looked elsewhere. The point was moot now.

Not that night. Not with Cord. No. She'd dropped her inhibitions and given into the need to finally experience their chemistry. Again and again. Thankfully, he'd been filled with the same need and had a ton of stamina. The amazing man had accommodated her wishes until she'd worn him out. But he'd fallen asleep in her arms with a smile on his face.

She'd had one on hers, too, and it grew as she'd listened to his steady breathing. It was so nice to see him relaxed for once, and not on alert like he seemed to be whenever he was awake. The guy walked around completely aware of his surroundings and everyone in it. Hell, he probably awoke at DEFCON 4 the second he cracked an eye open in the morning.

It was the reason she'd slipped out of his bed before dawn. One look at her and he would've noticed her uncertainty. Detected her worry and drilled her until she'd admitted her fear that the light of day might have changed his opinion of her prowess the night before. This would've led to unwanted questions about Drew. Or worse.

God, what if he'd awoken and declared the night a mistake like he had their first kiss?

No. There was no way she could've stayed. Her fledgling wings would've broken, and she would've died of mortification. And shame.

After Drew, she'd promised herself never again.

"You okay?" Cord asked, sledgehammer resting on his

shoulder, attention solely on her.

"Yeah." She nodded. "Why?"

His keen gaze narrowed. Great. He was doing his "Warlock" thing. "First, you looked like you wanted to strip me naked and lick chocolate off my body."

Damn. She inhaled deeply. Now she was never going to get that image out of her head.

"Then a second later, you looked like you were in pain."

All the pain was behind her, and she was determined to keep it that way. "No. I am thirsty, though." And hungry for something that probably wasn't good for her. And chocolate. Damn him. "We should take a break. Go hydrate." She motioned toward the house, suddenly in dire need of a cold drink.

He hesitated but finally glanced around at the fifty feet of fence they'd installed so far that day. "Yeah." He nodded. "I could use a drink." He dropped the sledgehammer with a *thud* before falling into step with her. "Some cold water sounds good about now."

Although she tried not to let it, the fact he was stringing a few sentences together and putting more words in them since his arrival last week, warmed her heart. Some of the old Cord was showing. And that, she decided, was definitely a good thing.

With lightness in her step, she entered the house and headed to the sink to wash up before grabbing two bottles of water from the fridge and handing one to Cord. He practically downed his in one gulp. The guy was even proficient when he drank water. She knew firsthand that proficiency followed through to the bedroom.

Memories of his aptitude brought heat to her face and places farther south. Good places where he'd bestowed his expertise. Her knees wobbled just thinking about it.

Damn, he was potent. Or was she pathetic?

Both. Definitely both.

After he crushed the air out of the bottle and tossed it in the garbage, he turned to find her watching him, and raised a brow. Great. He probably read all that on her face in one glance. Before he could grill her about which illicit idea she was entertaining now, she offered him the rest of her water. Heat entered his gaze, but instead of walking away and ignoring his wants like he usually did, he surprised her by stepping close until the bottle met his chest.

The air around them stilled while her heart beat out of control. In a slow, sure move, he reached for the bottle, but instead of removing it from her grasp, he wrapped his fingers around hers in a sensual move she felt clear to her core. So deep she trembled. And with that smoldering gaze boring deep, he placed his mouth on the rim and took what she offered. Finishing every last drop.

"Damn, Cord." Her voice came out breathy. "Now it's hotter in the house than outside."

"Not my fault," he claimed, letting go of the bottle but not her hand. The plastic bounced off the floor with a light, hollow *thud*. The complete opposite of the erratic pulse pounding in her ears. "It's your fault for not quenching my thirst."

She swallowed, watching his thumb caress her skin. "I gave you my water."

He cupped her face and held her gaze, his dark and full of the need consuming her body. "Not what I'm thirsting for." Then he was kissing her with a slow, thorough precision that had her toes curling in her boots and her good parts quivering.

Haley had no idea what changed, what prompted Cord to make the first move this time, but she wasn't complaining. Except maybe that they had on too much clothes. She snuck her hands under his shirt and brushed the ridges of his abs. God…he was hot. His skin was on fire and moving under her touch.

"So good," he mumbled after releasing her mouth to dip his head and kiss his way down her throat.

She let out a low moan in agreement and slid her hands up his arms, thrilling to the feel of his biceps hard beneath her fingers. "Every time." It got better and better. Or maybe it was because she'd been pent up since leaving his bed the other morning.

His breath was warm on her skin, and by the time his lips found her collarbone, she had mush for brains.

She cleared her throat, hoping it would clear her mind enough to hold onto a thought. "So…what is this?"

His soft chuckle huffed against her skin. "Think it's obvious."

"No, not that." She smacked his arm but didn't push him away. "Another night?"

He hoisted her up onto the counter. "How about a 'right now'?"

"Works for me." She'd barely gotten the words out of her mouth when he ripped the tank top over her head and tugged her bra straps down her arms.

"God, you're hot." Satisfaction glittering in his gaze, he trailed his hands up her ribs, stopping just below her breasts. "Damn hot."

She agreed with a sigh, and a second later, he captured her mouth in a delicious, wet kiss that had the pulse pounding loud in her ears. He was such a great kisser, but she needed more. Ever the mind reader, he cupped her aching breasts with his wonderfully callused hands and brushed his thumbs over her tight peaks. The combination had her moaning and hooking her legs around his hips to draw him closer.

A groan rumbled in his throat. He thrust against her, and she saw stars. How could he make her so hungry and needy so damn fast? Haley was about to encourage more when the sound of a car door slamming echoed in the distance.

Cord stilled. "You expecting company?"

Chapter Eleven

"Stone! Brick!" Haley hugged the bastards who had shit for timing, her delectable curves covered once again.

Disappointment rushed through Cord. Just when he'd finally given in—finally acknowledged Haley was no longer married, no longer beholden to Drew—and given himself permission to act on their passion that was far from quenched, his idiot friends show up.

To help out at the ranch.

Like him.

Damn. He needed to remind himself she hadn't invited him to the ranch to have sex. She needed help getting the place ready. The sex was an unexpected surprise.

Since the woman insisted on answering the door, and it *was* her door, Cord remained in the kitchen and let her handle things. Leaning his back against the counter, he folded his arms across his chest and watched his buddies take turns introducing their women.

When it came to his sister's introduction, Haley stilled before snapping her gaze his way.

"Brannigan? As in Cord Brannigan?" she asked, while her eyes remained fixed on him.

Lizzie smiled at him, as did the others. "Yep, he's my brother, and the only one who calls me Lizzie. So, please, call me Beth."

At that, Haley's mouth curved into a big grin. "Okay, Beth." She turned back to his sister and Brick. "I have got to hear how you handled that."

"Not well," Cord stated, pushing from the counter to head for the door behind them. He wasn't about to stand by while they talked about him as if he wasn't there. "It's time I got back to work."

The twinkle disappeared from Haley's eyes and her spine straightened. "Okay."

Now he felt like an ass. He liked when she smiled with her eyes. "You don't have to, though," he said. "Stay and visit."

"Cord's right," Stone said. "Brick and I will help him. We're here to pitch in."

Brick nodded. "You have us for two nights, and we'll be back again next weekend, too."

Haley blinked. "Oh, wow. I don't want to take you away from At-Ease. Especially for so long."

"No worries. Vince has it covered," Stone replied. "And Leo's pitching in more now, too. So it's all good."

Jovy slid her arm around Stone and smiled at Haley. "You're not going to get rid of them, so you may as well use the stubborn guys."

Cord grunted. Stubborn was definitely a Mitchum brothers trait.

Haley exhaled and an invisible weight appeared to lift from her shoulders. "Okay. I can really use the help. There's a lot on Cord's plate."

His? Surprise washed through him. She was the one who'd been toting the load for God knew how long. Between trying to keep her uncle's ranch going, to converting it into a new business, it was a wonder she was still sane. It proved her mettle. Admiration spread through his chest in a wave of warmth. She really was something else.

"Well, we'll clear some for him. Don't worry." Brick winked. "And if that's cornbread I smell, I'd be happy to clear that plate for you, too."

The light was back in Haley's eyes, sparking in her chocolate brown depths. Christ. A man could get lost in them. Drew had been a lucky son-of-a-bitch. And nearly fucked it up before he'd died.

"Yes." She grinned. "I baked it fresh this morning."

And the delicious aroma had tantalized him the minute they'd come in for water. But then his hunger had switched to something much more appetizing.

Brick rubbed his hands together and smiled. "I look forward to enjoying it at supper, after a good day's work."

"Thanks." Haley nodded then glanced at the girls. "I feel bad leaving you in here. Just make yourself at home."

Stone set his hand on Haley's shoulder. "Actually, why don't you stay here, too? Jovy is a killer business woman, and she's itching to talk to you about the business side of your boarding ranch."

"Yes." The pretty entrepreneur nodded, excitement gleaming in her eyes. "I'd love to take a look at your business plan and give you pointers. Help you get your books set up. Whatever you need."

Relief softened the corners of Haley's mouth and her body sagged, just a little. "Really? Lord knows I need help in that department."

"And I'd love to talk to you about your opening day," Lizzie stated. "I've got some inexpensive, fun ideas."

Haley divided her gaze between the two women and shook her head. "Wow. I…I don't know what to say."

"Say yes," Lizzie encouraged. "I don't believe you're as stubborn as my brother has led me to believe."

Shit.

A brown gaze collided with his. "Has he now?" She slowly smiled and warmth entered her eyes. "He's right. But, I'm also not stupid. No way am I turning away two people willing to help me tackle my least favorite chore. So, thank you both. Come on. The office is this way." Haley hooked her arms with his buddies' girlfriends as if she was indeed afraid they'd bolt.

Watching the three smiling women disappear into a room down the hall loosened something in Cord's chest. He had no idea what the hell it was, except it felt positive.

"You owe me twenty bucks, bro. Fork it over." Brick snapped his fingers, capturing Cord's attention.

He glanced at the brothers exchanging money and raised a brow. What the hell had they bet on now? Haley accepting help? Even he wasn't sure he would've made a wager.

"Never been happier to lose a bet." Stone glanced at him and grinned.

Shit. "You were betting on *me*? What the hell for?"

Stone shrugged. "Expected Warlock to hold out longer than a damn week."

Hold out? Damn. He knew where this was going. Fuck that. He pushed past the idiots and strode from the house.

Their chuckles followed.

Bastards.

"Can't outrun it, Cord," Stone said as he fell into step beside him.

Brick appeared at his other side. "Yeah. The jig is up. Cop to it."

"I'm not trying to outrun a damn thing," he muttered, coming to a halt near the unfinished fence. "Just needed to put some distance between you two idiots and Haley."

Brick backhanded his brother's chest. "Ah, that's sweet.

He's worried about Haley."

"That's how it starts," Stone said.

He narrowed his eyes. "What the fuck are you to talking about?"

A twitch tugged at Stone's lips. "You and Haley."

Ah hell. He muttered a curse. "There is no me and Haley."

"Don't even try to deny the two of you had sex. It's damn evident in the possessive way you look at her."

Possessive way? "That's bullshit," he grumbled.

"No. No, it's not," Brick said, and had the good sense not to smile. "You're in that confused stage. I get it. You want her but don't fucking want to want her."

"Yeah," Stone agreed. "Even though your mind screams at you to stay the hell away. You can't."

Damn. They were right. Still… "You're making too much out of this. We're just blowing off steam."

Stone's brow rose to disappear under his hair. "Does Haley know that?"

"Hell yeah," Cord said. "She's the one who initiated it."

Brick rubbed his jaw. "Hate to break it to you, pal, but given the history of your connection, it's a hell of a lot more than steam." He lifted the posthole digger from the ground and nodded at him. "Ever since Drew's death, the two of you have been dripping with sexual tension and tiptoeing around each other like an elephant in a damn minefield."

Anger heated Cord's veins in a fierce, swift wave. "I don't know what the hell you're talking about." He faced Brick, his fists clenching and unclenching. "She was married to Drew. I never would've done anything."

Brick held up his free hand and shook his head. "Hey, I never said you would."

Stone glared at his brother. "What my idiot brother is trying to say is that she's no longer married, and you two can do whatever the hell you like."

"Exactly," Brick said. "Life is too fucking short, and sometimes our stupid brotherhood code is just that. Stupid. You and I nearly fucked up the best damn thing to happen to me because of it. Don't make the same damn mistake, or be dumb enough to think it's just sex. It'll bite you on the ass."

He picked up his hammer. "I hear what you're saying, but back off. It was one night. We blew off some steam. I'm happy with my life the way it is."

For the most part that was true. Except if he'd arrived with more than three condoms in his pocket, then he would've had more than one night with the woman. It was the lack of protection that helped him fight his desire the rest of the week. Until an hour ago. With her watching him with that dark, hungry gaze—again—he was willing to go to plan B. The one where a condom wasn't required for what he'd had in mind.

"Bullshit." Brick leaned on the posthole digger and smirked. "You're not happy with having one night."

"Bullshit," he threw the words back at his friend. "I get it. You two are in committed relationships for the first time in your damn lives, but quit trying to fix me the fuck up."

"Look, Stone." Brick elbowed his brother while nodding toward him. "He's using his words."

Stone nodded, also regarding him closely. "I know, asshole. I was trying not to bring it to his attention."

Christ. "What the hell are you talking about now?"

Stone shrugged. "The fact this is the most you've talked to us in two years."

"Yeah," Brick said. "Your sentences have more than two words. Or a grunt."

Cord grunted, then flipped them the bird.

Stone smacked his brother's arm. "See what the hell you did?"

"I know." His buddy grinned. "But don't worry. Two weeks from now he'll be smiling all the time. And whistling, too. Remember how he used to whistle?"

"Yeah, that Skynyrd song about a bird," Stone replied with his own grin.

"I've got a bird for you." He flipped them both off again. "If you came here just to piss me off then go the hell home. I'll get Haley back out here. She's a hell of a lot more useful than you two asshats."

And a damn sight prettier.

"He's toast," Brick told Stone. "Maybe we *should* call her out here."

"Son-of-bitch." Cord clenched his fists and got right into Brick's face. "You going to flap your damn gums all day or put that energy into work? The fence isn't going to build itself."

The big idiot raised a brow. "You're nicer when she's around."

Christ. He was losing his touch. Used to be he had enemies and Rangers alike pissing themselves when he'd used that tone.

"Yep," Stone agreed, helping his brother start another section of fence. "I can hardly wait to see him next week."

Was it too late for a beer? Cord turned his back on them and returned to finish pounding nails in the post he'd left earlier.

"Me, too. Think he'll thank us for our present?"

"Hell yeah."

He refused to rise to their bait anymore. Fuck 'em. They could think whatever the hell they wanted. Conclude whatever the hell they wanted. He knew the truth. Haley was a friend, a naked friend, one he'd love to get naked with again. But that was it. Nothing more. She was looking for a corral fence, not a picket fence.

Two weeks from now he'd be heading back to At-Ease and his uncomplicated life in Joyful. He'd look back on his time here fondly, but that was it. He wouldn't miss it, or her. And he refused to dissect the reason his chest tightened at that thought.

Chapter Twelve

It'd been years since Haley had a fun girls' day. And even though the day had been spent discussing her least favorite things, like ledgers, account receivables and payables, and payroll, she'd pretty much had a smile on her face the whole time.

Jovy and Beth were a riot, and she got on with them instantly. It was refreshing not to be judged or pitied. Just accepted. It made setting up accounting programs and rearranging the office actually enjoyable.

"Are you kidding me about the cow?" Haley opened the desk drawer to shove a folder inside when her gaze caught on a copy of the divorce papers Drew had never signed. She needed to get rid of them.

The pretty brunette snorted. "I *wish* I was kidding."

Forbidding her mind to revisit that dark time, Haley shut the drawer, opened another, and dropped the folder. "Did she really stalk you?" she asked, refocusing on the conversation.

"Yeah," Jovy replied. "That mother heifer tried to run me off the road the other day. Thank God the fence held."

At the mention of fence, Haley's gaze strayed to the window, again. All afternoon it drifted to the great view of male testosterone in action. The Mitchum brothers were gorgeous, but it was Cord who captured and held her attention. And made her hot enough to squirm, remembering a time those competent hands had worked on her.

"That's some view," Beth remarked, gaze trained on the older Mitchum.

Jovy sighed. "Indeed. The only thing better would be if they were shirtless."

Holy hell, Haley's temperature skyrocketed just from the thought of seeing the rippling muscles she'd touched a few hours ago. "Not sure my heart could take it."

"Mine, either," Jovy remarked. "But I'd bring the popcorn."

Beth giggled. "And I'd grab the wine…and leave the ogling of my brother to the two of you."

Haley's laughter mixed with theirs. She probably should feel weirded out by *ogling* Beth's brother in the woman's presence, but since the friendly girl didn't seem to care, and the guy was going to be gone in a little over two weeks, she figured she should look while she could.

"You know, Haley." The woman turned to face her. "I need to thank you."

She frowned. "What for? You're the one who spent the afternoon helping me." Beth's ideas for the grand opening were smart and thrifty, involving a few local venders the woman insisted she'd call on Monday. "I should be thanking you."

Green eyes, the same shade as Cord's smiled at her. "But you've done something pretty amazing."

"Okay, now you've completely lost me."

"I'm talking about my brother," Beth replied. "Whatever you've been doing to him, for him, with him, whatever, please don't stop."

Haley stilled, but inside her heart thudded hard in her chest. "I haven't done anything, really." Except share a few amazing climaxes with the guy.

"Yes, you have, and it's made a difference," Beth insisted. "It may be subtle, but I've seen it."

"Me, too," Jovy said. "The tension around his lips is gone, same thing with his shoulders."

"And his eyes. They aren't as shadowed, you know?" Beth's own eyes filled with tears as she leaned forward to squeeze Haley's hand. "Whatever demons he brought back with him from that last deployment don't seem to have as tight a hold on him. And I'm forever grateful to you for helping him."

"But…" She shook her head, at a complete loss, her stomach clenching tight. The guys returned from deployment two years ago, and granted, she'd made a point not to see them because it stung, but that didn't mean she didn't care. "I'm sorry. I didn't know he was having problems. He hasn't said a word. I really didn't do anything."

"You're distracting him. Making him enjoy life. Trust me." Beth smiled, patting her hand before releasing her to sit back. "That's not just something, that's a big something."

Shoot. Haley sucked air into her tight chest. "I… All we did was spend one night together," she admitted. "Neither of us wanted more."

Liar. She so did. Still did.

Jovy raised a brow. "You don't want to spend another?"

"Yeah." Beth leaned closer. "Was once really enough? Because it certainly wasn't enough for me with Brick, although that was all it was supposed to be. And you seem to have that same look on your face I had walking around after my supposed only one-time thing with him."

"Me, too, with Stone," Jovy said. "I had that look of

complete satisfaction along with frustration, because it wasn't enough."

Damn. "Is that really how I look?" She rushed to check her reflection in the bathroom mirror down the hall.

Crud. They were right. Her gaze was kind of soft, and her mouth had this relaxed, almost goofy curve, while her shoulders were bunched tight.

Beth's and Jovy's reflections joined hers. Theirs were smiling.

"Face it, hon, you want more, and there's no shame in that."

"Exactly. And it doesn't have to mean rings." Jovy waved her hand and her gorgeous rock flashed under the lights. "But it can mean enjoyment. Why not take advantage of it while you can?"

"Yeah. My brother is stubborn. He thinks it's okay to deny himself fun. He's lived by this code his whole life, putting himself last, because he had me and my mom and our grandmother to worry about."

"A misguided sense his wishes didn't count." God, could she relate.

"Exactly," Beth said. "I'm finally getting him to realize I'm responsible for my own life. And to let me live it. Now, he needs to start living his and worrying about himself. But he's too damn stubborn to see it. Or do it. I'm hoping you'll help him."

"You mean persuade him to have fun?" Haley's heart rocked hard in her chest again as they walked back to the office.

"Yes, that's exactly what I mean." Beth nodded, retaking her seat. "The way he walked up to you today. The way your bodies automatically leaned into each other, there's trust and chemistry, and it's so great to see my brother connect with someone. I really hope you'll consider connecting some more.

Make him have fun. Go after what he wants. Not what he necessarily needs."

Jovy smiled. "And if they both happen to be the same, all the better."

"Okay, so…" Beth grimaced. "Talking about my brother having sex is gross, but I think you've got the picture."

"I don't know." She sank into her chair behind the desk. "I'm just starting to get back on my feet. Starting to enjoy life again. I wouldn't want him to get the wrong impression. Or to think I'm clingy."

Jovy snorted. "Trust me, that guy would love for you to cling and clutch and do all sorts of 'put your hands on his body' moves."

Beth groaned. "Thanks for that, Jovy. I just threw up in my mouth a little."

Heat rushed to Haley's cheeks and she groaned, too. "I can't believe I'm talking about this in front of his sister."

Beth shook her head. "I can't believe I'm talking about it, either."

Jovy chuckled. "Then you're both going to love this."

She tossed something onto the desk. A box of condoms slid to a stop in front of Haley.

Oh. My. God. She blinked and her mouth dropped open. "I…what—"

"You're welcome," Jovy replied as if Haley had thanked her. "Always remember to cover supply and demand. Last thing you need when you're about to demand he finish the deed is to have him run to the store for supplies."

The sound of the front door opening then closing and men's voices getting louder had Haley quickly opening a desk drawer to shove the box inside. As for her crimson face, there was no way she could slip that in the desk or she would've before three large men spilled into her office, making it feel smaller than a linen closet.

"Well, ladies, how goes the office set up?" Stone asked, stepping right over to Jovy and kissing his fiancée full on the lips.

Brick followed suit, treating Beth to the same attention, while Haley did her best not to give in to the urge to look at Cord, who stood in the doorway. She could feel his gaze on her, but she remained strong by staring at the desk.

That now housed a box of freaking condoms.

It felt like there was a big neon sign blaring out the fact they were in the top drawer. Condoms she was supposed to use with Cord. Heaven help her, that knowledge made her feel a little bit naughty, and a whole lot of parched. Good Lord, her face was hot. She needed water. Which of course brought to mind the bottle she'd shared with him…and the hot-as-hell kiss afterward.

Perhaps that box of condoms burning a hole in her desk wasn't such a bad idea after all.

...

By the time his sister and the rest of the gang drove off Sunday afternoon, Cord could tell Haley was pleased. Thing was, he had no idea if it was because of the progress they'd made on the ranch, or something else.

She kept smiling at him, shifting pieces around in his chest. The constant knocking, and rocking, and hammering proved he still had a heart, but he wasn't sure that was such a good thing. It stirred up shit. Some best left buried, and some that drove him bat-shit crazy. Like his damn attraction to her.

He wanted to touch her and taste her all the damn time. It was interfering with his thought process and messing with his mind. Although he was more than ready to pick up where they'd left off when they were interrupted last Friday. He'd sported a hard-on all damn weekend.

"You okay?" she asked, standing next to him on the porch, watching the truck disappear down the long drive, her sweet, citrusy fragrance doing nothing to lessen his condition.

Other than the Guinness book of hard-ons? "Fine. Why?"

"You look troubled."

His lips twitched. One word for it. "That's my middle name."

Amusement sparkled in her eyes. "And here I thought it was stubborn."

"That, too," he said, opening the door and standing back while she entered the house, his body heating with the brush of her curves.

"Well, Cord Troubled Stubborn Brannigan"—she smiled at him as she passed—"I like your sister. And I like how Brick is around her. They complement each other so well. It's really kind of sweet to see."

It was *now*. Not so much when he first found out.

Warm fingers curled around his bicep as they stood just inside the door. "But how are you with it all?"

"Me?" No one had really asked him that before. He was kind of at a loss. An extremely new state to him. It even cooled his libido a few notches.

She squeezed his arm. "I'm not going to tell anyone, so you can be honest. Talk to me about it."

He didn't talk about his feelings. Ever. Well, except during the group therapy thing. Which he missed this week with the arrival of Brick and Stone. They'd all missed it. But outside of it? Hell no.

So why was it, when he gazed into her warm whiskey-colored eyes, he forgot to not talk?

"I'm good. Now," he replied, and meant it. "Did they tell you I punched Brick when I found out?"

"That's how any of you would've reacted. But I'm not interested in them. I'm asking you. Your thoughts are what matter to me. It had to be hard to realize your sister was dating Romeo, ladies' man of the Ranger Rifle Team."

Damn. How the hell was he supposed to react to that? The fact warmth flooded his chest and his heart swelled wasn't something he wanted to acknowledge, either.

"And I'm not surprised you punched him," she continued quietly, removing her hand, and he was surprised at how he instantly missed her touch. "All those years you kept your sister away from the guys because you didn't want her to get involved with a military man. You didn't want her to have that kind of life. The kind I had. And it was a tough life. It was also good at times, too. But it was a decision I made. Right, wrong, or indifferent, it boiled down to it being my decision, so the same would've held true for Beth."

He nodded. "I know." Now.

"Then you also know none of that mattered. Brick wasn't in the Rangers when he and Beth met."

"No, but he was supposed to head to Vegas to work for the commander in his security company."

Haley's brow rose before she nodded. "Guns. Bullets. Danger."

"Exactly. But truthfully, even that had been off the table by the time I found out about those two. So I was basically a controlling ass." And why the hell did he tell her that? He huffed a breath and moved away from her. She was zapping his brain cells right and left, and making him act irrationally.

"Wow." She followed him.

Ah hell.

"I didn't think I'd ever hear you admit that."

"Didn't think I'd ever say it, and if you tell anyone, I'll deny it." He tried to give her a stern look, but his lips twitched in response to the twinkle in her eyes.

Witch.

"Don't worry, Warlock. Your secret is safe with me."

Secret? "What secret?" He hated secrets.

"That you're human," she replied, sliding a palm up his chest to cup his chin.

What the hell was it about her touch that made him feel so alive? He leaned into it.

"And I really like this human side of you." Then she lifted up on tiptoe and brushed her lips to his.

The rest of his brain cells joined the zapped ones while she slowly drank, and nipped, and skimmed his lower lip with her tongue. Once again, as he was about to grab her and deepen the kiss, she released him and stepped back.

"Sorry." Haley blinked and shook her head, as though maybe she didn't know what she was doing, either. "You blur my brain sometimes, Cord."

"No need to apologize. I wasn't complaining. If I remember correctly, we have unfinished business."

She opened her mouth to reply when something behind him caught her eye, and a second later her laughter filled the air. "Oh, wow. I…um…"

He turned to find out what had her so flustered, and muttered a few curses when he spotted the box of condoms on the counter with his name written on them in Brick's handwriting. "I'm gonna kill him."

Chapter Thirteen

"I'd rather we thanked him," Haley said, heat and amusement evident in her tone.

He twisted around to face her, his mind completely blank, since all the blood in his body rushed to parts south. "Come again?"

"I'd love to."

Hell yeah.

He chuckled and stepped toward her. "That can be arranged." A thrill ran through him when she didn't try to move away.

"Thanks to your friend." She palmed his chest, while he set his hands on her hips. "And Jovy," she added.

Jovy?

He reeled back. "What makes you think these are from her, too?"

"Oh, not those." Haley's smile widened. "I'm talking about the ones in my desk drawer."

Friday afternoon immediately came to mind when he and the guys had finished for the day and walked into her office.

She'd sat there behind her desk with a pretty flush on her face that stole his breath. But now he knew why she wouldn't make eye contact.

"I'm guessing they wanted to make sure they had you covered."

He laughed at her pun and dipped down to run his lips up her throat to the soft spot behind her ear he knew drove her mad. "I like how *you* cover me," he murmured, and captured her indrawn breath in the hot, wet, deep kiss he'd wanted to take since their interruption at the kitchen counter Friday morning.

When he drew back for air, he slid his hands to the bottom of her tank top and tugged it up over her head, groaning at the sight of her breasts barely contained in the lacey bra. Then he reached for her shorts, slipping his fingers behind the waistband, gliding across her quivering belly to pop the button.

"So, I guess this means we're using the condoms?" She ran her hands up his biceps, brushing her thumbs over his muscles.

He never knew a simple touch could be so erotic.

"We're using the condoms." His heart pounded in time with her zipper as he drew the metal downward and released to watch her shorts fall to her feet.

She stepped out of them and stood before him in lace and black combat boots.

"Damn, Haley, you're beautiful." Fire raced through his veins and he pulsed with need. Still, even in his lust-induced state, he wanted to be sure they were on the same page. "We both know what this is and what this isn't, right?"

"Right," she replied. "We have an expiration date. You're leaving when this boarding ranch opens."

"Exactly." He lifted her up, and she wrapped her legs around his hips so he could carry her to the kitchen. He set her on the island near the condoms. "We can enjoy ourselves in the meantime." Skimming his hands down her hot curves, he heard his own groan echo between them. He dipped his head to her breasts, which were now spilling out of her bra.

Haley's gasp of pleasure ricocheted through him. He wanted more. Needed more. He indeed knew what this was and what this wasn't. This wasn't just for Haley; it was for him, too. He needed to touch her. To feel her. To lose himself inside her, but he also needed to be touched by her, to experience the crazy consuming fire with her. He needed to connect again.

Cupping both lace-covered breasts, he nuzzled them and trailed kisses to one of the tips budded tight behind the lace. Delectable. He slipped his tongue underneath and rasped over the nipple before sucking it into his mouth.

"Cord." She inhaled sharply and held his head in place.

"Right here," he murmured against her soft skin as he switched to the other side.

Her moan rumbled straight through him, making him harder than the granite under her sweet ass. He reached behind her to unhook her bra and tugged it down her arms as he drew back to watch the bounce of sweet freedom. Before he could voice his pleasure, she held his face and leaned closer to kiss his temple, and followed down his cheek to the length of his jaw with soft, sensual, little kisses.

Next, she tortured him with slow brushes toward his mouth then hovered over his lips, sharing the same air, and he found himself holding his breath. She was killing him. Waiting, anticipating for her to cover his mouth, he remained still, very still, but she touched down on his other cheek, ripping a groan of frustration from his throat.

"Haley, damn it." He grasped her upper arms, two seconds away from taking what he wanted. Which also happened to be what he needed—her mouth on his.

"Hmm?" she murmured against his cheek.

"Kiss me."

She chuckled against his jaw. "So demanding."

Before he acted on that want, she captured his mouth for a kiss that rocked his world. The light brushes she'd treated his face to were gone. She thrust her fingers in his hair and ransacked his mind and body with a hungry, demanding, thorough kiss. Her greedy moans reinforced the need in her tasting and nibbling and sucking, which matched the fierce hunger gripping his body tight. By the time they pulled apart to suck in desperately needed oxygen, his ears were ringing.

He set his hands on either side of her on the island and leaned in to brush his lips up her throat, thrilling at the feel of her body trembling under his lips. "You know payback's a bitch, right?"

Lifting her head, she held his gaze prisoner with her own deep brown one. "God, I hope so."

Her smile was earnest and the hottest thing he'd ever seen. His heart squeezed. She was unlike any woman he'd ever known. Strong, with a vulnerable edge. Hot, with a sweet nature. And she'd been hurt. She was a survivor, and Cord had promised himself to keep his hands off her because she'd been through shit and deserved better than a guy who was emotionally challenged and held himself back. But he gave in last week—nearly twice—and now, once again, he was unable to resist her pull. He was also beginning to realize he wasn't any of those negative things in her arms, and she was more than happy with what he offered. She didn't want forever. She wanted right now. Wanted to be taken out of herself and transported by unbearable pleasure.

Well, hell. He could deliver that.

Her long, supple legs were wrapped around him, those killer boots locked across his ass, and she used them to pull him in close as she rocked against him when they were kissing. This afforded him a view that had his heart rocking in his chest. Her matching lace panties were pulled tight against her sweetness, showcasing every delectable fold.

"Damn, you're a vision." He traced the lace with the pad of his finger, and satisfaction warmed his blood when she jumped and gripped his upper arms. So he did it again, brushing the edge of her panties, finding them wet.

She moaned his name and rocked closer.

"Lift up," he urged, and tugged her panties off, leaving her naked, except for her boots, and trembling. His two favorite things.

She let out a shaky breath. Running his hands up her legs, he leaned in and captured her mouth for a heated kiss, brushing his tongue to hers, loving how she moaned in his mouth and pressed closer. She was soft and warm and trusting in his arms, and it filled him with an unexpected joy like he'd never known. He released her mouth and lowered his head to place open-mouthed kisses across the full curve of a breast.

She gripped him tight and then clutched at his arms, her fingers sinking into the muscle of his bicep. He skimmed his thumb across her nipple, and she whispered his name.

"Tell me," he said, skimming his other hand up her inner thigh.

"That. Yes."

"What?"

"More of that, Cord. Now. Please."

He smiled. "So demanding."

She choked out a laugh and punched his arm, then sucked in a breath when his other thumb brushed her center. Then he dropped to his knees, because he wanted to taste her and make her cry out his name.

His heart stopped at his eye-level view of heaven. Caressing her legs, he nudged them wider, and his insides fisted with a fierce, almost painful need. Turning his head, he kissed one inner thigh and then the other, touching his tongue lightly on her skin until she moaned and shoved her fingers in his hair again.

"So gorgeous," he whispered against her heated flesh, and ran his hands to her hips to tug her to the edge of the counter where he met her sweetness with his tongue.

"Cord." She gasped and held his head, making the sexiest little needy sounds that throbbed all the way to his tip.

Over and over, he explored and learned what she liked and what she loved, and what she really, *really* loved. Before long, Haley released his hair to grip the counter again and arch into him, panting and moaning, her head thrown back, sweet curves bouncing in her wild abandon, a goddess worthy of worship. And he did, paying her homage, taking her right over the edge she so enthusiastically sought. He loved that she trusted him and gave him everything, holding nothing back when she came with a throaty moan and his name on her lips.

He nearly burst from the raw need and sheer joy—not just from *her*—but in *him* as well.

Chapter Fourteen

When Haley returned to planet Earth, she opened her eyes to find Cord standing in front of her, shedding his clothes.

Damn.

She'd barely gotten her breath, was quivering with aftershocks, and her body was already responding to his magnificent naked form. When the last of his clothes met hers on the floor, she reached behind her for the box of condoms and removed a packet, all while her gaze stayed on him.

He drew near, gloriously naked and proud, and as he held her gaze, she lifted the packed to her mouth and ripped it open with her teeth.

With a muffled curse mixed with a growl, he took the condom from her hand and rolled it on before she could protest, having wanted the do the honors.

"I'd never last if you touched me," he admitted, as if reading her mind. His voice was as strained as the condom. Then he was between her legs, his body on fire and hard, and because the island was a little too high for comfort, he scooped her up.

The feel of his muscles moving beneath her as he walked with her arms around his neck, her breasts rubbing his chest, legs wrapped around his hips, it was almost enough to set her off.

She whispered it in his ear before biting his shoulder.

With a low oath, Cord halted in the middle of the hall and pressed her back against the wall before aligning his tip with her center, and then, eyes on her, he pushed inside in one sure thrust.

Haley cried out, vaguely aware he'd muttered her name as well, the exquisite feel of him filling her too incredible to keep quiet.

"Always so damn good," he uttered against her mouth, letting out the sexiest male groan of approval she'd ever heard when he pulled nearly all the way out and pushed back in. "So damn good." Desire was thick in his gravelly voice, and his words were nearly as arousing as his thrusts.

Everything he did was just right. His touches, kisses, caresses, thrusts, all of it propelled her forward toward the edge. She wondered briefly how he could have her there again so soon, but it didn't matter. Nothing did but the fact she wasn't the only one in this crazy, hot grip of passion.

He drove into her over and over, his smoldering gaze now glued to hers, his eyes glittering like prized emeralds. She got the impression he liked the sound of his name on her lips.

Then he shifted her leg higher on his hip, changing the angle, pushing deeper, making her gasp. She went a little wild then, bucking, arching into him, feeling him everywhere.

He held her on the edge, and she was completely lost in him, lost in the exquisite, hot pleasure he showered on her. And as he slid a hand between them, brushing his thumb over her center, he proceeded to take her right out of herself with shocking precision. As a million sensations wracked her body in another mind-blowing orgasm, he gripped her hips and pushed into her hard, shuddering as he followed her over that blissful edge.

...

Cord awoke in the middle of the night, heart pounding in his chest as the usual Drew nightmare that forced him awake slowly faded into the darkness of the room. His room.

At Haley's ranch.

Shit. Immediately aware of the soft, warm, naked body curved around him, he was grateful this dream hadn't ended up with him sitting bolt upright in bed. But considering her dead husband was the subject, he needed air.

Quiet and careful, he extracted himself out from under Haley, halting at the side of the bed when she murmured a protest in her sleep.

When she appeared to settle down, he slipped out of the room and headed toward the kitchen for water. Nightmares always parched his throat. He hadn't had any in a while. They usually only happened now when they were triggered, and sleeping with his dead buddy's widow was a definite trigger. His gut tightened as he pushed back the guilt. If he had to guess, the only reason he hadn't had one the first night they spent together was because she'd worn him out and he'd been too tired to even think straight.

Tonight, though, he'd been a pansy-ass lightweight, falling asleep after their second round. Images flashed through his mind of their incredible off-the-wall sex, then their long, erotic-as-hell shower afterward, and how painstakingly slow they dried each other off before burning up the sheets in his bed.

His legs were still finding their strength.

Attempting to shake off the adrenaline—and guilt—he walked silently through the kitchen and opened the fridge.

With a muffled oath, he swiped a bottle of water from the top shelf and sucked it down in under ten seconds.

Drew had died a day after Cord had found the guy cheating on Haley. As far as he was concerned, he didn't owe the unfaithful man his loyalty anymore. It wasn't a crime if he and Haley enjoyed a few hours in each other's arms. They deserved the enjoyment. No reason to feel guilty.

And yet, he did.

But that wasn't the whole reason why, a voice whispered in his head, and he pushed that to the back recesses of his mind, too.

The empty bottle he tossed in the recycling bin landed with a soft *thud*.

"You okay?" Haley asked sleepily behind him.

Chapter Fifteen

Cord turned and noted how the soft glow from the light above the sink cast shadows over her breathtaking silhouette. Standing there in his shirt and nothing else, the resilient, sexy woman interfered with his breathing. And the thing was she had no idea how much she affected him.

When he didn't answer, she frowned and stepped closer. "Cord?" Her gaze raked over him and returned to meet his with a spark of heat. "You felt like taking a midnight stroll... naked?"

He lifted a shoulder. "Just thirsty. I'm fine now."

Her eyes continued to regard him closely. Christ. He resisted the urge to shift his feet. Now he knew what the others went through at the opposite end of his gaze. She raised a brow.

"It's true." He pointed to her garbage. "See for yourself."

Still holding his gaze, she stepped to his side before looking down into the bin. "Do you need something stronger?"

"No. Thanks." He hadn't expected that question.

She reached out and set a hand on his arm. "Do you want

to talk about it?"

"About what? My water?"

She stroked his bicep. "No. Your nightmare. Do you have them often?"

He stilled, and his heart lunged into his gut before returning to pound the hell out of his chest. Her gaze was sure and strong and full of understanding. Ah hell. She thought he was suffering from a flashback. "Not unless they're triggered."

Dawning entered her gaze and she released him to step away. And because he didn't like the look of reproach dimming her eyes, he reached out to grasp her arm.

"Don't," he said quietly.

"Don't what? Let my dead husband come between us?" She met his gaze and shrugged. "Looks like he already did."

"No," he said, still holding her arm. "You're no longer married to Drew. He's dead."

"I know that." She cocked her head. "I just wasn't sure you did."

"I wouldn't have touched you if I hadn't, and I'm pretty sure the same goes for you."

She nodded, and he felt her body relax under his hand.

"My nightmare had nothing to do with you." It was all him and his guilt, so in essence, it wasn't a lie.

Tell her the truth, his mind insisted. It was the perfect lead in, but he didn't want to mess with her head or ruin her fond memories of her time with Drew. What good would telling her about her husband's affair do her now? None.

Christ. This guilt fucking sucked. He was losing his mind. Possibly his heart, too.

"Okay." She shifted closer and set her palm on his chest. "Let's go back to bed." Her fingers slowly trailed down his torso to stroke his abs and venture south.

This battle of guilt versus desire raged inside him, with his desire for Haley winning out. It was too strong. And she was waiting for his reply. He answered by scooping her up and capturing her laughter with his mouth.

Bed. The best way to rid his body of the adrenaline coursing through his veins…and the need he harbored for the woman that he couldn't seem to quench.

...

None of the Rangers had returned unharmed from the op that had taken Drew's life. It had been evident to Haley during that very first visit after his death two years ago, and even more evident last night.

Finding Cord standing in her kitchen stark naked in the middle of the night with a haunted look in his eyes was enough proof something was eating him up.

Guilt.

God, she hoped it wasn't about Drew, but she suspected her late husband was part of it. If so, there wasn't anything she could do. Cord would never let her. In fact, sleeping with her was probably part of that guilt.

And that sucked. Neither of them owed her late husband anything, but she wasn't about to tell Cord about Drew's infidelity. She didn't want to ruin the memories he had of his buddy, to shatter the respect he and the other Rangers harbored for a man they loved and served with. It was in the past. It didn't matter now.

She hated being helpless. That was exactly how she'd felt staring into his troubled gaze last night. Thankfully, she'd been able to lure him back to bed. A rush of heat flooded her body and put a smile on her lips. The deliciously attentive man had been too occupied to let anything else invade his thoughts but taking care of her. And he'd taken care of her all night long. So well, in fact, she'd slept in. Something she hadn't done in years.

Cord had left her with a smile on her face and no energy in her naked body. He'd pulled the covers up and kissed her temple, urging her to go back to sleep. Too deliciously exhausted from their round three at dawn, she did as he suggested and rolled over for a few extra minutes of shut eye. Which turned into two whole hours and the reason she was running late that morning.

The sound of a vehicle pulling up sent her into action. Great, his sister was here already. Haley quickly threw on clothes and laced up her boots, then rushed into the hall, pulling her hair back into a ponytail.

"Hi, Beth. Come on in," she greeted the smiling woman, taken aback once again at how much the woman's eyes were like Cord's, except perpetually happy.

A pang rippled through her chest. She could remember, years ago, how his eyes weren't so shadowed. Closed up. Dim.

What she wouldn't give to see that pleased expression on his face more often. It surfaced once in a while and had been present the other day at the high school where he kicked her butt at the games. His body had been relaxed and a smile remained on his face most of the day. Telling him about Drew would put the darkness back in his eyes. Their fun day had proved the old Cord was still in there. She wanted him to be that way all the time. She wanted that for him so bad, Haley vowed to make that her mission. By the time the man returned to At-Ease, he was going to be at ease with himself. Smile more. Laugh more. Joke more. Lighten the hell up.

"I was just about to put some coffee on," she said, leading the woman into the kitchen.

"Perfect. That'll go great with these." Beth set a bag on the island. "Vince sent them."

Haley stilled. "Cannoli?" It couldn't be. She glanced inside the bag and smiled. "Oh my God. I can't believe he remembered. It's my favorite." Capicola made the best cannoli she'd ever tasted. It was melt-in-your-mouth goodness she hadn't had in years.

"He said it was and made sure to save you some from last night's dinner."

"I was going to make some pancakes, but to hell with that. I'm having cannoli for breakfast." She grinned as she put on a pot of coffee and grabbed two plates. "I hope I'm not eating alone, though. I won't feel so guilty."

Beth grinned. "If I must. Far be it for me to let you walk on the wild side of breakfast alone."

She laughed. "I appreciate the sacrifice."

The next half hour, over coffee and cannoli, Haley and Beth talked about their childhoods, and their conversation reiterated things that made sense about Cord.

He'd already told her about the death of his father when he was a teenager, but Beth went into it in more detail, explaining how he'd stepped up to take on the responsibility of helping his mother and grandmother and watching out for his sister. Responsibility was important to him, and the fact he wasn't frivolous with his wants. It was ingrained in him to take care of others. Especially family. Family came first. Family meant everything to him.

The men he served with were his family.

Drew was his family.

But who took care of Cord?

Her heart broke a little for him, but she'd never let him know that. The last thing the independent man would want was anyone feeling sorry for him.

"What did Cord do for fun when he was growing up?"

"Boss me around." Beth sighed. "Seriously, he didn't. He had part-time jobs after school, then joined the Army right after graduation."

She frowned. "Didn't he date?"

His sister shrugged. "Yeah, but nothing serious. He was

too caught up in taking care of me and my mom and my grandmother, he had no room for another woman in his life," Beth said. "But if there's anything else you'd like to know about him, ask away." The woman winked as she bit into her second cannoli.

The allure of having a pipeline into the enigmatic Warlock's past was almost too incredible to pass up, but it still kind of felt wrong, so she sighed. "I'd better not. Somehow the bugger would know."

Beth snorted. "True. God, I hate when he does that. I couldn't get away with anything growing up."

Haley smiled, her heart going out to the teenage Beth. "That had to really suck."

"Oh, it did. Big time. But I understand why he was so protective. I just wished he would've let me live my life. Make my own mistakes. Stumble and learn to right myself."

"You seem to have done all right for yourself," she pointed out, feeling a weird need to defend the well-meaning control freak.

"I have, but that's because I decided to go out and do what I wanted without checking with Cord first. Or letting him know until after the fact."

Haley snorted. "Love it. Ask for forgiveness, not permission."

"Exactly." Beth grinned, reaching for her coffee. "Speaking of permission, I contacted everyone on our list and they all enthusiastically jumped at the chance to set up tents here during that Sunday of your grand opening weekend."

"What?" She stilled. "All of them? There were twenty-two vendors on that list."

"I know. And they all want in. They really loved the idea, and they're excited to have you join their business community."

She sat dumbfounded, just staring at the smiling woman.

"How did you ever pull that off?"

Beth chuckled. "I'd love to take the credit, but it all goes to you. They were thrilled that you wanted to continue to contribute to the local economy."

"Wow." She sat back in her chair and blinked again. "I don't know what to say."

"I do. Good job, Haley." Beth reached out to pat her hand. "You work hard and are fair, people around here notice that. You should be proud of it. Own it."

"Thanks. I'm not used to that type of recognition." Or compliments. Drew had hated the long hours she'd put into the cattle ranch. But he'd been deployed half the time, and it had become her life. It was hard to let it drop and travel around the world with him, so she eventually stopped.

"Well, it's deserving, so get used to it," Beth said firmly, sounding so much like her brother it made Haley smile.

"Thanks," she repeated, then stood. "How about I give you a tour so you know exactly what Haley's Haven is about?"

After a quick cleanup, she grabbed a bottle of water from the fridge and led Beth out the door. Excitement rushed through her veins, and she knew it wasn't just from getting to show her friend her new dream. It had to do with a certain Ranger who had put his life on hold to help her out, in more ways than one.

She was looking forward to *helping* him out later, too.

He was pretty serious about working. But the place was ahead of schedule, thanks to the Mitchums helping Cord out over the weekend. And since they were due out the upcoming weekend, maybe she could persuade the man to slow down a little.

When they were alone.

Chapter Sixteen

Cord knew Haley was approaching even before he heard her talking to his sister. His whole body shifted to alert mode. Awareness trickled through him in a heated, tingling sensation that twitched his favorite body part to life.

How the hell could he still be hungry for her? Especially after enjoying breakfast in bed that morning. Damn, he was hopeless. A smile tugged at his lips. Yeah, hopelessly in lust with the woman. She revved his engine like no other. Somehow, their second night had topped their first. Each time got better and better and did nothing to lessen his appetite for the responsive, giving, and demanding woman.

"And last but not least, this is the old barn. I've nicknamed it Old Redder for obvious reasons." Haley's voice drifted to him, along with his sister's laughter. "Cord has been working hard in here, repairing long neglected issues. Right now, he's working on the stalls, hopefully ridding them of all things spider and critter related."

Lizzie's presence helped curb his appetite. Last thing he needed was his sister catching sight of his *condition*. Christ, she'd turn his self-indulgence with Haley into a relationship, and his mother would catch wind and have him married off before he could blink.

"I hate spiders, or anything with more than two legs, unless it's a dog, cat, or horse," Lizzie said, and he could picture disgust wrinkling her forehead. "My brother is an ace spider remover. He had a lot of practice with me."

He exited the stall. "Hey, Lizzie," he greeted, pulling his sister in for a hug as he smiled at Haley. She had this soft look about her face that said she'd been thoroughly satisfied and wasn't going to apologize for it. Well, neither was he.

He struggled with the notion that maybe he should give her a hug as well, after all, she'd given him a hell of a lot more than that a few hours ago. But he didn't want his sister to get the wrong impression, so he let his gaze linger on her a little longer before releasing his sister.

"Lizzie's right," he said, nodding to Haley when she handed him a bottle of water, and ignoring his sister's pleased grin. "She was forever giving me a damn heart attack with her screams while growing up. I remember this one time, I found her on the kitchen counter, trying to scale the refrigerator because there was a tiny spider on the floor."

"It was a jumper."

"Eww." Haley shivered, running her hands up and down her arms, exactly like his sister. "They're the worst."

Hiding a smile, he uncapped the bottle and drank the water while listening to the women.

"Tell that to my brother." Lizzie grimaced. "He was highly agitated with my suggestion of removal."

He snorted. "Burning the house down was not an option."

"Why not?" His sister blinked, totally serious. "If it has twice as many limbs as me, it has to go."

"Sounds reasonable to me," Haley stated, with a lift of her shoulder.

He knew when he was outnumbered. And right now, he was definitely outnumbered. He shook his head and set his empty bottle down against the outside wall of the stall. "Well, you'll be pleased to know that, up to this point, all spiders have been removed."

"Super, then we can stay right here." Lizzie smiled. "The place looks really great, and from what you've told me, and the plans I've seen, it's going to be a wonderful place for people to board their horses."

He nodded, pride washing through his chest, but not for him, for Haley. It was her idea. Her dream, and she was making it a reality. He was just a worker doing what he was told. She was the one who planned, researched, then planned some more, and was now making it all a reality. "It was all Haley."

Lizzie nodded. "She's something else."

"I know," he said, gaze trained on the woman whose chest rose as her lips parted and warmth flooded her incredible brown gaze.

God, she was beautiful. He liked that look on her. He liked it a lot.

"Well, I'd better get going," Lizzie announced. "I have a few things to take care of now that we have a vender count and I've seen the layout."

He forced himself to transfer his attention to his sister. "Okay. We'll see you this weekend."

"Oh, right, about that." Lizzie blinked. "The guys wanted me to tell you they have an inspection late Friday, so they thought they'd stick around At-Ease and make the session, since they missed it last week. So we'd come out first thing Saturday morning. Is that okay?"

"Of course," Haley replied, then glanced at him. "You should attend the session, too. I feel bad you all missed it last week because of me."

"Hey." He stepped close, despite his sister's presence. "It wasn't because of you."

"Cord, you were all here laying the fences *I* needed done by next week. Of course it was because of me."

He shook his head. "The sessions aren't mandatory and we don't always make them, isn't that right, Lizzie?"

"Yes." His sister nodded. "Cord's right. They don't go to them every week."

He noted Haley's relieved breath before she nodded, too. "Just promise me you'll make this week's, okay?"

It was his turn to nod. "Okay."

"All right, I'm going to get going. Thanks for the coffee and the tour."

He watched his sister pull Haley in for a quick hug before she waved to him and left. "Sounds like Lizzie's got some good plans for your opening."

Haley's warm smile returned. "Yeah, can you believe she got all twenty-two venders to agree to show up and man a table? She's a miracle worker."

"So are you."

"Me? I haven't done anything. You're the one busting your ass."

She didn't see. Her humility humbled him at times. He'd never really met anyone like her, outside of Lizzie and Jovy. Haley had always been special, and the more he was around her, the more he realized there were a lot of facets to her, too.

He was impressed with each of them.

"So, Cord, my spider-slayer, critter remover, orgasm creator extraordinaire, tell me something?" She set her hands on his chest and slowly pushed him backward into the stall he'd vacated.

He knew he had work to do. It wasn't something he'd ever strayed from, but his body was calling the shots now.

"Anything." He'd tell her fucking anything if she kept

looking at him like he was the special of the day and she was famished.

She leaned in to kiss a path to his ear. "I was wondering…" Her soft lips pulled his lobe into her warm mouth and sucked.

His dick went from alert to active duty in a split second as all the blood rushed to help with maneuverers. "Anything," he repeated, running his hands over her hips and around her ass and pulled her in tight.

"Mmm…" Her breath was warm on his neck and sent shivers racing down his spine. "With you, the possibilities are endless." She ran a hand down his chest, then abs before, holy shit, she dropped to her knees and unbuttoned his jeans. "Since you had breakfast in bed, can I have lunch in the barn?"

He sucked in a breath as she freed him. "I shouldn't…I have work to do."

"From the looks of it, so do I." She smiled wickedly up at him as she leaned in and took a long lick of his throbbing erection.

His world tilted. Ah hell, that felt good. Reaching out for something to hold, he set his hands on her head.

"Correction," she muttered against his length. "There's enough here for breakfast and lunch. I'm going to have *brunch* in the barn."

He chuckled, but then choked on an inhale when her warm mouth closed around him. Fuck, yeah. His head *thunked* against the stall wall as he closed his eyes and wrapped his hand around her ponytail.

Maybe he had time for a quick brunch.

• • •

By the time Thursday night rolled around, Cord noticed a significant change in Haley. She smiled more, laughed more, joked more often. Her exuberance was contagious, and lack of inhibition was a gift. All week, they worked side by side but stopped to enjoy each other whenever the whim hit them. Which was often and everywhere. Old Redder. The new barn. The arena. Front porch swing. Just about every room in the house. And his personal favorite, right now in the back yard with a million stars as a backdrop to the goddess who had just ridden him until they were both gasping for breath and completely spent.

He watched her resting on top of him, her ragged breaths warm on his chest where he held her against him. His hands were full of her soft, supple curves that were still trembling with aftershocks. She brushed her thumb back and forth across his chest, her light strokes keeping time with her inhales. The woman was killing him without even realizing it. She concentrated on her task, her sole focus on her breathing, and he knew firsthand how engrossed she got in the details. Damn, he really loved when he was her sole focus.

Tightening his hold, he kissed her head. "You were amazing."

"Mmm…" She kissed his chest. "You, too, cowboy."

She was like the night air surrounding them…fresh, warm, and welcoming. So unselfish and giving. But they'd shared more than work and their bodies that week. She'd opened up and talked about her childhood.

Surprisingly, so had he. By rights, it should've freaked him the hell out how easily she got him to talk about his past, his family. But it felt right and natural, and gave him the opening to ask her questions. For the first time in his life, he wanted to get to know more about the woman in his bed. But she wasn't just any woman, not that there were many, this was Haley, the woman he'd admired for over half a decade. His desire to know everything about her grew each day. He wanted to know more.

Rubbing his palm up and down her arm, he decided to give it a shot now. "It's so peaceful here."

"I know." Her contentment washed over him.

He decided to push further. "How did you come to live with your uncle? I know you're mom died when you were younger, but what about your father? You don't talk about him."

She stiffened for a beat then relaxed. "My mom kicked him out after she discovered he had a girlfriend on the side."

Damn. Cord's insides fisted tight. Her own husband had cheated, too.

"I'm sorry," he said. The news reiterated he was doing the right thing by keeping that knowledge to himself.

"Me, too," she replied, still stroking his chest. "I stayed with my aunt, then my mother's other sister, until my uncle took me in."

Her father leaving. Mother dying. His gut twisted just thinking about the young girl being shipped off to stay with one relative after another, until her uncle had stepped up to take her in. God, she must've felt so alone. He could relate to being raised by a single mother, but at least he'd also had his sister, and he talked about that with Haley without even realizing he was opening up.

It hadn't felt like such a bad thing. In fact, it had felt good. Damn good. And each time they talked, he opened up just a little more, especially noticing when he did, she followed suit. And that was his goal. To help Haley. He wanted to bring that sparkle back to her eyes. To show her support, something he realized, she'd severely lacked in her life. He basked in her progress. He felt good for her and wanted to continue to help her.

Not just for her, but for him, too. It was weird, but her triumphs felt like they were his, no matter how small. He wanted to share them with her. Wanted to share his with her, too.

So he decided to do just that. "I know it's short notice, but do you want to come to At-Ease with me tomorrow night? I'd like to show you around the ranch. I'm sure the others—"

"I'd love to," she cut him off, lifting up to smile one of her special, brilliant ones that warmed him from the inside out. Soft hands slid to his shoulders and her thumbs brushed the sides of his neck. "Thanks for asking."

Then she was kissing him, and he could feel her elation in that kiss, feel her open up and share even more of herself, when he had no idea there was more of her to share. And son-of-a-bitch it was addicting. He wanted more. He wanted to do things to make her this happy all the damn time.

When she broke the kiss, he didn't release her, happy to have his arms around her. "You should pack an overnight bag, just in case we get tied up after the session. Unless you'd rather we come back here?"

She shook her head. "No, I'd like to stay the night."

He kissed her nose. "Good." Then he swatted her ass. "But we'd better put in a good day tomorrow. Boss Lady might not let us go if we're not finished."

She laughed. "Yeah, I heard she can be a real bitch."

He chuckled. "I heard that, too."

"Hey." She smacked his shoulder. "So is payback."

Adrenaline rushed through his veins. "Yeah? Bring it."

The thrilled that flashed through her eyes sent a reciprocating one through his already invigorated body.

"Oh, I will," she said, challenge and mischief resonating in her warm tone. "Trouble is, you're not going to know when."

Alert mode activated…in a good way, he was energized, happy, and feeling more alive than he had in years. Being around Haley brought him back to life. He didn't know how it had happened, or exactly when, but it had, and now he couldn't imagine going back to just existing once Haley's

Haven opened. It was unfamiliar territory.

"Could be tonight," she said, dipping down to brush her lips across his chest. "Could be next week, could be two months from now."

Two months? Did that mean she wanted to continue to see him after his work there was through? He waited to see if it was a slip of the tongue and she was going to try to take it back. The fact he held his breath because he didn't want her to take it back was an eye opener for him. Guilt flooded his stomach. Not something he wanted to think about right now. Not with the woman letting her guard down, and so open and relaxed in his arms.

He buried the guilt and tightened his hold on her. "Bring it," he repeated. "We've got all the time in the world."

Was he actually considering a relationship?

That required trust. Did he have it in him?

"You're on," she replied, shifting closer.

His gaze strayed from the stars above to the beautiful woman snuggling against him, humming a Lynyrd Skynyrd tune. Maybe the more important question was did *she* have it in *her*?

Chapter Seventeen

Haley hadn't been this eager in years. Happiness and enthusiasm mixed to keep her in a constant state of excitement all night and day. But most of all, she was touched. Touched that the incredible man driving them through Joyful—a town she'd always meant to visit but never had—dropped his defenses and asked her to join him.

This was a big deal for him. Haley knew this to the bottom of her soul, and the thing was her acceptance had been just as big a deal. And he knew that, too. They were both making big strides in joining the land of the living again. What had started out as a desire to help him find his smile turned into a journey that had them both gaining much more.

As he pointed out different things about his town, she could hear his heart in his words, and knew that in order to be able to she had to be listening with hers.

"It seems peaceful here."

"It is." He turned off the main drag and drove down a quiet country road surrounded by fenced off fields with an occasional homestead and a cow or two.

Wait. She turned in her seat to glance out his window. "Are any of those Lula Belle?"

Smiling, he pointed to a black-and-white cow grazing near the fence a few hundred feet ahead. He slowed down. "That's Stone's girlfriend there."

The cute thing had big brown eyes that blinked as they passed. "She looks sweet."

He chuckled. "She is, to everyone but Jovy."

Haley laughed. "That's so crazy."

"I know, but it's true," he insisted. "So much so, they're thinking about having her at their wedding."

She snapped her gaze to him. "What?"

His smile widened. "She's more than likely going to crash it, so Jovy thinks they should just invite her."

"Oh my God." She laughed. "I really can't wait for this wedding."

"I know." He turned onto a private road, driving underneath a large metal arch with the words At-Ease welded in the middle. "It's going to either be epic or an epic failure; either way it'll be interesting to see."

He'd be done working on her ranch by then.

The flutter in her stomach reached into her chest. What had started out as a need for shared physical release somehow turned into a much deeper connection with the amazing man who was steering more than the truck. He had control of her happiness...and her heart. There was nothing carefree and light about what she felt for Cord. And she suspected he felt the same. But what if he didn't?

He wouldn't have asked you here if he didn't, her mind insisted. She liked to listen to her mind. It was usually right. And he would've corrected her last night after her stupid post-orgasm brain threatened payback could happen two months from now—well past their expiration date.

Cord reached across the console to lace their fingers

together. The unexpected action touched her almost as much as his invitation. It was as if he needed to touch her, to connect with her before they arrived at the place he'd put his heart into.

She squeezed his hand to let him know she understood and felt it, too.

The ranch came into view a second later, and it was beautiful. Huge, yet peaceful. The buildings were spread out, each with their own space so it didn't feel like they crowded each other. And all of it was surrounded by open fields of wild flowers and several large oak trees.

"Wow, this place is amazing," she gushed, shaking her head in awe.

The main house was a beautiful two-story with a large front porch where Jovy and Beth were sitting, enjoying a glass of wine. She felt Cord stiffen before he released her hand and parked next to a green truck.

It was nice while it lasted.

She got out and exchanged greetings with the women, then lost her train of thought when Cord came over to re-lace their fingers. In front of the women. In front of his sister.

His gesture shocked her silent and sent warmth streaming into her chest. This was a huge step. For both of them.

"Hi, Lizzie. Jovy." His tone held a bit of challenge, daring the women to remark about the obvious implication of their handholding.

Both women were too busy wearing pleased expressions, and Haley knew they were much too smart to jeopardize it with questions.

Stone stepped out onto the porch and stopped dead when his gaze fell to their linked hands. The sudden stop sent Brick plowing into his brother with a curse.

"What the hell, bro?" Brick's frown transformed into a huge grin the instant his gaze spotted their connected hands.

She glanced at Cord and spoke low enough for only his ears. "I think you've effectively shocked everyone here." Including her.

"Just want them to know where things stood."

She wished she knew, and wanted to ask but not in front of their audience. "Well, you really know how to silence a crowd."

His lips twitched. "You should see my encore."

She chuckled. "Looking forward to it."

"How about a tour first?"

Joy spread through her and curved her lips. "I'd love one."

At-Ease was as amazing as Haley had suspected, but seeing it through Cord's eyes, feeling what it meant to him to be a part of something so wonderful, was an honor she would never forget.

"How many does one barracks hold?" she asked outside the women's quarters.

"There's a capacity for twelve in here," he replied, running his hand lightly over the wooden doorframe, his chin up and shoulders back while pride emanated in his emerald gaze. "The men's has more because we installed a barracks section as well as the six private quarters with bathrooms and lifts for those who need them. It's important to us to cover all bases so we won't have to turn anyone away."

His open, earnest gaze matched the honesty in his tone, and her throat heated in response to his passion for the veterans.

The incredible man more than touched her heart; he held it in both hands. This meant she couldn't keep it safe or protect it. But when he walked her past the men's barracks and into a barn full of horses and told her to pick one out to ride, she forgot about her misgivings.

Forgot everything except how much she missed riding Gypsy. It was as if he knew this.

"Ride? Really?" she asked, her heart rocking in her chest. It'd been so long since she'd been on a horse.

"Yes," he replied, gaze softening, no doubt from the stupid tears that filled her eyes.

Inhaling, she glanced around, noting every horse was beautiful, but for some reason, she was drawn to a gorgeous chestnut mare. Haley stepped toward the beauty and let her sniff her hand. "This one." She ran her fingertips gently over the name on the stall. "Cayenne."

When Cord didn't immediately reply, she glanced at him to find a strange look on his face, but it disappeared in the blink of an eye. Ten minutes later, she was galloping across fields atop Cayenne while Cord rode a gorgeous paint named Galahad. She wasn't surprised by his riding prowess. The man was good at everything, and by the time they returned to the barn and dismounted nearly an hour later, she added "and *with* everything" to his list of attributes. The horses gravitated toward him. They were excellent judges of character and obviously trusted Cord.

She did, too.

Trust was a powerful and wonderful thing. And damn important to Haley. He was something else. His compassion for the veterans and passion to help them, along with his love for his family and friends, stole her breath.

She'd never look at him the same again. He was always special to her, but now he was just…more.

Everything.

And she suddenly wondered if she would be enough.

"Hey," he said, stepping toward her, after leaving the horses in the care of one of the veterans. "What's wrong?"

"I… This place is amazing." She couldn't imagine him anywhere else, even though the past week she had thought he'd seemed happy at her ranch. It wasn't the same. It wouldn't be enough. She wouldn't be enough. It didn't contain his heart and soul like this place. "I'm just…in awe."

He stared at her a moment then squeezed her hand. "*You* are amazing, and *I* am in awe."

God, how did he do that? How did he know her fears? Know what she needed to hear?

She blinked the stupid burning from her eyes and squeezed back. She longed to kiss him but knew he wasn't ready to show that type of affection at the ranch by the way he'd refrained from doing it since they'd arrived. "You are sweet."

"Sweet?" He looked pained. "I'd rather be hot."

She laughed. "Well, you are that, too."

"That's better," he said, tucking her into his side as he walked her to the side door of the main ranch house. At least he wasn't afraid to touch her. "No more talk of sweet around this place. I have a reputation to uphold."

"Okay, sugar," she replied as he opened the door and ushered her inside a huge kitchen where one of her favorite people stood slicing carrots.

"Haley!" The second Capicola caught sight of her, he set his knife down and stalked over to pull her into a hug. "How are you? Thanks for the saltwater taffy. It's what I miss most about Jersey."

She hugged him back. "God bless the internet. It was the least I could do for your incredible cannoli."

"I'm always happy to give you my cannoli," Vince said, waggling his eyebrows. "But the way Warlock is staring me down, I might have to get his permission first."

"Hell no." She cocked her head and bounced her gaze between Cord and Vince. "Nothing and no one comes between me and your cannoli."

Vince laughed, pulling her in for another hug. "It's so great to see you again. I've missed your smart mouth."

Smiling, she drew back and winked. "And I've missed

your cannoli."

"Okay." Cord stepped forward to drape his arm around her shoulder. "We've already established that."

She smiled as he led her out of the kitchen, then gave her a quick tour of the house before he grabbed their things from the truck and took them up to his room. Butterflies fluttered low in her belly at the thought of staying in his room with him. It was different than staying in his room at her house. This was his house. His actual room. And knowing how private Cord was, she knew staying with him was a big thing.

It sure as hell was for her.

With supreme effort, she tried her best to keep the pure joy from her face as they joined the others on the front porch. This time Leo was there, too.

"Haley," he said, stepping close to give her a hug. His gaze was dark, but not so much troubled as concerned. "How have you been?"

Happy that he'd initiated the move, she kissed his cheek and drew back. "Pretty good, thanks to Cord." And she meant that in a lot of ways.

"Hey, what are we?" Brick groused. "Chopped liver?"

"Forget it, bro." Stone winked at her. "I don't think she was referring to the ranch."

She glanced at Cord, who'd gone silent at her side, but she was relieved to find him smiling. "Actually, if I take the ranch out of my answer, then I am great thanks to Cord."

Something warm and fierce flashed through his gaze, and she decided she really liked how that made her feel. Important to him. Yeah, she really liked how that felt.

"That's great to hear," Brick said. "But how *is* the ranch coming along?"

Cord reached for her hand and entwined their fingers, again. "It's coming along good, and after this weekend, I think we'll have the major issues taken care of."

True. Once they finished the fence this weekend, and the company she'd contracted came out next week to build the riding arenas, she only had small things on her list. Excitement raced through her veins. It was almost done.

Could've been done a lot sooner, her mind whispered. Yeah, if she'd used the money Drew left her. But she couldn't bring herself to touch it. Every time she considered it, the thought twisted her gut. It felt like compensation for his cheating. Cheating money. She'd manage without it.

"Well, we should get inside to set up," Leo said, heading for the door.

Brick kissed Beth, while Stone laid one on Jovy, or was that the other way around? Haley wasn't sure.

"See you in later." Cord brushed her palm with his thumb, sending her pulse into orbit. He glanced at their smiling audience, the women in particular, and narrowed his gaze. "Behave." Then he released her to turn and disappear into the house with the Mitchums.

A second later, she was sitting in a chair with a glass of wine in her hand between the two grinning women. "So...that just happened. Right? I mean, I didn't imagine any of this." She reached out to touch Jovy. "You are real, right?"

"Yes." The dark haired woman nodded. "You're not dreaming."

"Thank you, Haley." Beth set a hand on her arm. "I can't believe it. Every time we see him, he changes even more." Warm green eyes filled with tears. "Thank you. I can't even say it's like having my brother back, because he's never been this happy. This content."

Now her eyes were filling with tears. Dammit. She swiped the wetness from her face, then sipped her wine. Okay, gulped, she gulped her wine. But dammit, she needed it. "I... We're just enjoying each other's company." But it was more than that. He seemed to want more, and she did, too.

"Well, I think it's safe to say he definitely enjoys yours." Jovy patted her other arm. "Just the fact you're here speaks volumes."

Haley agreed. Their friendship had grown into something much stronger over the past few weeks. And their fun turned into something serious and meaningful, as well.

Beth nodded. "Yeah, especially if he asked you."

"He did." God, she would never invite herself.

Both Beth and Jovy sniffed.

"That's huge." His sister finally gave up and let her tears flow. "Thank you," she said for the third time.

She drew in a shaky breath. "I'm getting just as much out of this…whatever this is between us. Trust me."

"So, what happens next?" Jovy asked.

Haley shrugged. "Damned if I know."

Beth frowned. "Do you really think you two can just walk away when your boarding ranch is open?"

No way. Not now. Not with all these darn feelings surfacing.

"I know I can't," she answered honestly. "But I can't speak for your brother."

"He'll be sadly mistaken if he thinks he can." Beth shook her head and sipped her wine. "He's stubborn, but hopefully not *that* stupid."

"Men are usually clueless when it comes to matters of the heart." Jovy sighed. "Especially if they're not used to using that organ."

Beth burst out laughing, and she and Jovy joined in. And as the conversation turned to Jovy's upcoming wedding, a bell sounded in the distance.

A cowbell?

"Here comes your rival, right on time, Jovy," Beth stated

Haley turned around, and sure enough, the black-and-white cow Cord had pointed out on the drive over approached.

"She comes here often?"

"Yep." Jovy lifted her glass in a salute. "Sorry, *sweetheart*, you're wasting your time, he's in a meeting."

The cow mooed but continued to amble toward the porch.

"Did you hear me, Lula Belle?" Jovy set her glass down on the table next to her and frowned. "He's inside."

At this, they received a shorter moo. Haley smiled.

"Guessing she doesn't care," Beth said. "I think she's here to see you."

"Me? Well she better behave or she won't be in the wedding party."

Lula Belle stepped up onto the porch and promptly knocked over Jovy's glass.

"Hey, you big cow," Jovy said. "You could've broken it. Be careful."

Haley bit her lip, trying not to laugh as she watched the cow lick the spilt wine. "Can cows have wine?"

Beth chuckled. "Apparently."

"Stop that," Jovy admonished. "You're going to get sick."

The cow ignored her.

"I'm serious. You won't even be *invited* to the wedding," Jovy threatened.

Lula Belled lifted her head and burped.

"Oh my God." Beth laughed and Haley joined in.

Everything they told her about the cow was true. She was freaking hilarious.

"Nice, Lula Belle. Very ladylike." Jovy shook her head, but Haley noted amusement in the woman's eyes. "No one in the wedding party is allowed to burp at the wedding."

Lula Belle backed off the porch and ambled away.

"She's a piece of work," Haley said, watching the cow disappear around the side of the house.

"Welcome to my life." Jovy smiled. "It's never boring."

Beth lifted her glass. "I concur. You're marrying Stone

and his girlfriend. Apparently, they're a package deal."

Jovy chuckled. "I know, but he's worth it."

Haley couldn't help but feel a little envious of the two women. All she knew was she liked being with Cord, and he appeared to like being with her. This felt different than it had with Drew. Cord didn't keep secrets. She just worried about his guilt. Hopefully he'd be able to let it go, where Drew was concerned. If not, this amazing path she was on would end up like Jovy's spilt wine. A waste of a good thing.

Chapter Eighteen

Cord lost count of how many times the guys kept glancing at him during the session. It was quite comical. He even smiled a time or two, which only seemed to garner even stranger looks. It got to the point where the therapist came right out and asked what was going on.

Cord grinned. "Got me."

"It's that." Brick pointed to him. "He's smiling."

"I've smiled before."

"Yeah, but not like all-the-time constantly," Stone said.

He snorted. "I don't smile constantly." He was quite positive he had a completely different look on his face when he was buried deep inside Haley.

"See?" Brick pointed again. "It's still there."

"And that's a bad thing?" the therapist asked.

Good question. Cord folded his arms across his chest and listened as the men debated the answer. When five minutes had passed and the session hadn't moved on to someone else, he decided to speak up again. "I had a good week. End of story."

"Don't you mean a great one?" Stone corrected.

"And I'd like to talk about the fact you let her ride Cayenne," Brick said. "You'd never let us ride your horse."

"Damn straight." He unfolded his arms but didn't elaborate.

"So you trust her?" the therapist asked.

Cord turned his attention to the man and nodded. "Yes. I do."

Saying it out loud cemented the admission in his head. He did trust Haley. Explicitly. She'd never betray him. She'd always have his back.

Leo smiled. "According to Haley, you had a *great* week."

"Actually, Haley said *she* had a great week, thanks to Cord."

And the straight-shooter Stone struck again.

Leo turned to Stone. "Isn't that the same thing?"

Holy fucking shit. Cord transferred his gaze from face to face until he finally met one who was just as baffled by everyone's interest in his love life. Vince. At least his Jersey buddy understood the fact that him smiling was no big deal.

Once the circus quieted down, the meeting got back on track. Christ, if he had known he was going to stir up so much shit, he would've stayed home.

Cord stilled. Wait. He *was* home.

Since when did he start thinking of Haley's ranch as home?

An hour later, as he folded his chair and carried it to the stack by the wall, he contemplated the after-session ritual. A beer usually hit the spot. Not tonight. He was more interested in the woman entering the rec room with Jovy and his sister. Haley glanced around the still crowded room, and the instant her gaze landed on him her expression softened. Heated.

Damn. Each of those expressions ricocheted through him with the intensity of a live round. Because he felt alive.

Especially when she walked straight for him, oblivious to the appreciative glances from some of the men, and the curious ones from their friends. No doubt, they wanted to see if he'd hold back, like he usually did. Even the therapist was hovering in the doorway, gaze trained on him.

Whatever.

He didn't owe anyone anything. Wasn't there to entertain. His only concern was for the woman approaching him with warmth and hope in her gaze that said she only wanted him. It sparked those primal needs to protect and worship again. Needs only Haley conjured. He'd never had those needs or urges before.

You love her.

The thought whispered through his mind, and instead of scaring the shit out of him, it made him feel good. It made sense. Of course he did. Christ, he'd been in love with her for years.

"Everything okay?" She frowned as she stopped in front of him, her brown eyes wide with concern.

"Great," he replied, deliberately using the analogy she'd stated on the porch. "Everything's great now that you're here."

A brilliant smile curved her lips and shone from her eyes. "I'm glad."

Needing to touch her to connect to the sweet, vibrant woman, he reached for her hand again. He wanted more, a hell of a lot more. If they were at her ranch they'd already be naked. But they were at At-Ease, in the middle of the semi-crowded rec room. So, even though he wanted to kiss her until they were out of breath, it was out of the question if the others were going to gawk at them like they were the main event. "Did you make any plans with the girls?"

She blinked. "No. We just talked over a glass of wine, which Jovy shared with Lula Belle."

"What?" He laughed.

"Yeah." She smiled. "Lula Belle showed up, knocked Jovy's glass over, and licked the wine."

"Well, maybe she's calling a truce," he said.

"Could be." She smiled. "And I didn't make any plans, why?"

He brought their entwined hands up to his chest and held her gaze. "Because I want you."

Her chest rose on a sharp inhale, but she somehow managed to keep it quiet, as if she could tell he was trying not to attract attention. "I want you, too, Cord. So much."

It was his turn to inhale quietly. He wasn't as good as her. By this time, only a few people were lingering about, so he got lucky it went unnoticed. But in truth, he was past caring. She wanted him. He was so done. "Come on." He tugged her to the other side of the room, where his sister and Brick sat on the couch near Jovy, Stone, Vince, and Leo. "Good night," he stated and didn't wait for a reply.

He squeezed her hand and led her to the stairs, not rising to the bait as the guys commented on their departure.

"Aw, look, Stone, they're holding hands again."

"I know. They grow up so fast."

Apparently it was true, because normally he would've flipped them a double bird, but that would require letting go of Haley's hand. Not happening. He wanted the connection. *Needed* the connection. She was more important than sparring with those idiots.

When they entered his room, he shut the door and pulled her right into his arms, taking the kiss he wanted to enjoy — away from prying eyes — the whole damn night. Cupping her face with one hand, he brushed her lower lip with his thumb before leaning in to slowly follow the movement with his mouth.

A soft sigh escaped her lips as he kissed one corner, then the other, then full on. She fisted his shirt and made the sexiest little sounds, brushing his lip with her tongue, causing his heart to pound hard in his chest. Slow and thorough, he made long passes with his, taking his time to kiss her with a lazy intensity that grew hotter each second.

And her taste? God, she was sweet and hot and hungry. So damn hungry that his own desire answered in kind. She nipped and drank and sucked, making him nuts. When they broke apart to drag in air, she held his face and smiled.

"Thanks for asking me to come here with you." Her breath was warm on his skin, almost as warm as her gaze. "I'm glad I waited until now to come."

"Why?"

She tenderly kissed his temple then down his face to pepper a few more across his jaw. "Because it meant something to you. And that meant something to me."

Emotions swarmed in his chest. He set his forehead to hers and stared into her heated dark eyes. "I want you," he repeated, a feeling of liberation racing through him. Having gotten the words out the first time downstairs, he wanted to keep telling her.

"You have me. All of me."

He'd wanted to get his hands on all of Haley since that afternoon when they were painting the barn door, teasing and tempting each other. Hell, his "want" for her went back a lot further, since…always. He wanted to touch her and kiss her, hold her and make her cry out his name. God, he loved hearing his name on her lips in a voice full of raw pleasure. Just thinking about it made him harder than hell.

Taking his time, he trailed kisses all over her body as he slowly stripped off their clothes. When they were both naked and drawing in air, he urged her to sit on his bed, then he nudged her until her back hit his mattress. Damn, she was a vision. She looked amazing, fucking amazing sprawled out on top of his covers, her gaze smoldering with intense longing, so dark they appeared black. He dropped to his knees before her and ran his hands up her legs. His insides fisted when he found her wet and warm.

She moaned and opened her legs wider for him, giving him a view that rocked his heart. Damn, he loved a woman who knew what she wanted. He'd never deny her wants. Never. He kissed a path up her inner thigh, sucking on a patch of skin while he slid a finger inside her. She gasped and shoved her fingers into his hair as if afraid he'd leave before she was ready.

Hell no. He blew on her and stroked deeper, wanting to hear his name on her lips as she came apart. Knowing her rhythm, he worked her with long, slow strokes, bringing her to the edge, his body breaking out in a sweat at the sound of her moans as she bucked into him. And when she tightened her hands in his hair, he added his tongue to the mix, giving her what she wanted, what he wanted, too. He took her over the edge, and she burst for him, with his name echoing off the walls in her sexy, throaty cry.

When he surged to his feet, she was still shuddering, staring at him with immense satisfaction glowing in her eyes. She lifted up on her elbows, her gorgeous breasts bouncing in tandem as she smiled at him. Sweet and hot.

"Is it my turn?" she asked.

He frowned down at her. "I thought that's what that was?"

"Oh, it totally was." She sighed. "But I meant my turn to get my mouth on you."

Chapter Nineteen

Cord grabbed a condom from his discarded jeans and rolled it on. "I wouldn't last two seconds with your mouth on me right now." And he wanted to last longer. He had plans. "Scoot back," he said and helped, grasping Haley's ankles and pushing her all the way onto the bed.

Then he worshipped her, starting at those ankles and making a slow journey up the wonderland that was Haley. Paying special attention to the curve of her hip, her breast, her delectable tips, loving her gasps and how her hands roamed over him on their own journey.

By the time his mouth found hers, she was trembling beneath him, making those noises he loved to hear. He needed more. He needed everything.

With their fingers laced together, he set their hands on either side of her head, he held her smoldering gaze and pushed inside her in a slow, sure slide that had them both sucking in a breath of raw, sheer pleasure.

Nothing ever felt better than being buried deep inside Haley. Not one damn thing.

"Cord…" Her eyes were full of everything he felt, and he drowned in her fierce, deep, whisky-colored gaze.

"Me, too."

He felt it, felt it all to the depths of his soul and his guarded heart. With his needs and his wants blurring, he dipped down to connect with her everywhere, kissing her hard and deep as he began to move.

His body was on fire and aware, and it was fucking powerful. He'd never felt so engulfed. So needed. So wanted. So loved. He thrust into her, and everything began to make sense. There'd been no time for his indulgences in his life. Sure, he'd enjoyed an occasional fling, but he'd never sought a relationship. None of them affected him deeply. Not like Haley. Never like Haley.

He never would've pursued this if Drew were alive. But once he let go of his restraint, it'd happened in an instant. Their bond, their crazy connection, had strengthened with time, and now he didn't want to be without her. He always wanted to be with her, always wanted some sort of connection. Whether they talked, or touched, or kissed hot and heavy or slow and sweet, or he was buried deep inside her warm, welcoming heat, she made him feel alive and held the darkness inside him at bay. With Haley, he yearned for things. The things he saw in her eyes: home, family, love.

She gave him that, willingly.

With her mouth moving under his, her body soft and warm, he had it all with her. It was real. And amazing.

"Haley," he murmured, when they broke for air and she kissed each of his shoulders with soft tiny brushes of her lips.

"I love your freckles," she murmured, her hands gliding up and down his back, ripping a groan from his chest.

He wanted to worship her some more, but their need was starting to take over. She wrapped her legs around his hips and he sank in even farther.

"Cord." She arched into him, eyes closed, head back, lips parted, with a fierce craving etched on her face.

He kissed her throat then nuzzled the curve of her neck. She gasped, tightening on him. Tightening everywhere at once. Fire shot through his veins. And when she did it a second time, he closed his eyes and let it all engulf him. The feel of her, their scent, his name on her lips.

It was everything. And still, he wanted more.

Slipping his arms beneath her, he drew her with him as he leaned back on his shins. Fuck, yeah. This. This was what he'd needed. What he'd wanted.

"Oh…damn…Cord," she choked out on a gasp as he slid deeper.

Her body was hot and trembling against his, everything connecting. She went a little crazy, rocking into each thrust, crying out as he gripped her hips and guided her movements, driving deeper, then deeper still.

She was brushing him everywhere, arms and legs banded around him, lush breasts with those gorgeous tight peaks grazing his chest, mouth open on his, saying his name over and over. Nothing separated them, not even air. They touched everywhere, and then she was coming, her sweet warmth gripping him like a vise while shuddering in his arms. It was too good. Too damn good. He gave up his control and let her guide him as she barreled right over the edge and took him with her.

Everything around him disappeared except for her. Her hungry gaze. Her cries. Her slick heat. Her trembling. Just Haley. Only Haley. That was the only thought in his head. Everything else disappeared.

His need to remain in control or unaffected. His trust issues even vanished, because he trusted Haley. Trusted her with everything, his body, his heart, his soul. And dammit, it felt good. So damn good…

She deserves better. Drew's words echoed in Cord's head. And he agreed, but he wasn't strong enough to ignore his wants anymore. And he wanted Haley in his life. Bad. He just hoped she felt the same when he eventually found the courage to tell her the truth about Drew.

• • •

For two days, Haley walked around with her head in the clouds, and she didn't want to come down, because, hell, it was great up there. She never felt happier or alive or more cherished in her life. She wasn't sure what exactly had happened, but Cord seemed to have come to some kind of decision or realization about them—about *her*—because when he touched her or looked at her now it was with everything in him.

And God, she couldn't get enough. Could never even have imagined she'd ever feel so lighthearted and free. Free from the pain of her past. From now on, she was only looking ahead. Only looking at Cord.

"Well, that should be the last of it," Stone said as he and Brick and Cord approached her porch where she sat with Jovy and Beth.

All afternoon, they'd had a great view of the men building her fence. In fact the view had been so great, she and the girls had settled in their chairs and watched the show for a good two hours.

"It's a shame," Jovy responded, running her hand over her fiancé's chest as he leaned down to kiss her temple.

"What is?" Stone straightened with a frown. "That we're done?"

Jovy nodded. "Yep."

"Yeah." Beth sighed, gaze eating up her man as he drew near.

"Damn shame," Haley agreed. "But at least we got

through some of that paperwork that was piling up."

"True." Jovy turned toward her. "The preliminary is always a pain. It should be just normal day to day stuff for you from now on."

"Good. I like normal day to day."

"Me, too." Cord stepped up to her and smiled as he accepted the drink she offered. Tonight, she was going to come right out and talk to him about continuing to see him after the ranch opened for business next weekend.

Right now, though, there was something else she wanted to discuss. With all of them. She waited until the guys found a seat and a drink before sharing her idea. "Since you all have a moment, I'd like your opinion."

Cord covered her hand she had resting on the arm of her chair and smiled. "What do you need?"

Brick lifted a brow. "On what?"

"I'd like to know your thoughts about me possibly hiring a few veterans to permanently help out around here."

She watched the surprise and delight cross each of their faces and relief rushed through her veins. She didn't want them to think she was trying to steal anything from At-Ease.

"That's an incredible idea," Cord said quietly next to her, bringing their joined hands to his lips.

"Yes. It's brilliant," Jovy gushed.

Stone nodded. "Drew would've loved this idea."

Everything inside Haley stilled and her heart hurt for the guys, because their friend wasn't as noble as they thought. She had to be careful. No way would she let them find out. So she nodded and forced a smile.

"I know several veterans who would probably jump at the chance," Cord stated.

"Then here's my next question." She met each of their interested gazes, letting the adrenaline vibrate through her and wash away her anxiety over Drew. "What do you think about me building either a bunkhouse for them, or maybe a few separate little cabins? I kind of like the cabin idea. It'll give them more privacy."

"Wow." Beth's brows rose. "That would be amazing."

"Where were you thinking?" Cord asked, pulling her to her feet to point out at the land. "Over by the north pasture?"

She nodded. "Yes." Not surprised he was already on the same page as her. "The well isn't too far from Pete's cabin, so I thought maybe the electricity and stuff would be nearby, too."

Stone and Brick glanced out at the land and nodded.

"After talking with some of the veterans this weekend, and watching them, I noticed how a few enjoyed working around the horses. It sparked the idea."

Cord slid his arms around her from behind and pulled her back against his chest. "You're amazing, you know that?"

"No. I'm not." She shook her head. "I just want to help. And I could use the help. Why not hire them? I'm sure you could recommend the ones you think would work out."

The six of them walked the land then went inside and spent a few hours sketching up impromptu blueprints and coming up with a feasible plan. Since she was also hiring a few kids from the 4-H Club, they figured she should hire two full-time veterans to start, basing it off the number of horses she had signed up so far. As the number of boarders increased, she would increase her employees accordingly.

The tricky part would be the construction noise and trying not to spook the horses.

But all in all, it felt right, and she was happy, happier than she'd ever been in her whole life, and that scared her to death. Because anytime she got too comfortable, or too content with her life, it was turned on its ear. Never failed.

Chapter Twenty

If Cord had doubted his feelings for Haley before, he was sure of them now. He loved the woman. She was giving and generous, and his chest was full with a mixture of pride and emotions brewing inside for the special woman.

Yesterday, she'd blown everyone away with her idea to hire veterans to work on her ranch. Her unselfishness was refreshing.

"There you are." She smiled at the sight of him as she walked out onto the porch, wearing nothing but his shirt.

He automatically reached for her as she neared, and sighed when she wrapped her arms around him. The sun was starting to set and it cast a warm glow over Haley's Haven. Tomorrow the company she'd hired to work on the arenas was due to arrive first thing in the morning. Not much was left but a few minor fixes.

"This place looks amazing, Cord." She tightened her arms around him. "Thank you so much for all you've done."

"It was all you," he said truthfully. "I added a little muscle that was all. You had the vision. And the drive."

"Cord?"

"Yeah?"

"Any chance you'll still come down to see me when you go back to At-Ease?"

His heart knocked into his ribs and a smile spread across his face. "Oh, I'd say there's a very good chance." He dipped down to kiss her neck and then shoulder. "This connection between us has gone way beyond the light and carefree thing we started a few weeks ago."

She turned in his arm to smile at him. "I agree. I was just afraid you didn't want—"

"Oh, I want, Haley. I want very, very much." He brushed her lips with his while he spoke and her body melted against him.

"Good to know," she replied, kissing him while she spoke. "Because I like being with you. I like having you around the ranch, and most of all, I like having you."

He cupped her face with both hands and held her open, honest, emotion-filled gaze. "I like when you have me, too. And I very much like having you around me."

When she gasped, he took advantage of her open mouth and kissed her long and deep, amazed at how much his body wanted her again, but it'd already been an hour. That was much too long to go without her sweet sighs.

Drawing back, he kissed her head. "Too bad we used up the last condom." He was going to have to make a trip into town.

She kissed his chin while her hand ran down his body to trace his erection through his jeans. "No we didn't. I still have that box from Jovy in the top drawer of my desk, remember?"

A smile tugged his lips. "That's right. I did forget about those." He cupped her sweet ass, groaning at the feel of her bare skin as he drew her against him. "Save's me a trip into town."

Her low chuckle warmed his neck. "Yes it does." Then she nipped at him and soothed the spot with her tongue.

Everything inside him tightened. "Hold that thought," he practically growled. He strode through the house and into her office, his mind centered on the woman waiting for him on the porch. The woman wearing his shirt and nothing else.

He loved that she wanted to wear his things, like maybe she wanted to feel him even if he wasn't there. A smile spread across his face, and his chest warmed. He was going to make a point to leave a few of his shirts behind.

Reaching for her desk, he opened the top drawers until he found the box of condoms. Pulling it out, his heart lurched at the sight of the document underneath.

Divorce decree?

Son-of-a-bitch. Haley had been divorcing Drew?

His gaze skimmed the date and his blood ran cold. During their last deployment.

He sank down into the chair and stared at the paper as if maybe he were seeing things. Reading it wrong. Getting it wrong.

But it was there in black and white. She had filed for divorce. And even though he knew firsthand she'd had just cause, never in a million years did he peg her as the kind of woman who would stoop to divorcing her deployed husband.

Damn. Was that why Drew had been acting so off? Preoccupied?

Maybe it hadn't been his threat to expose the guy if he didn't come clean to Haley after the mission. Christ. He'd been living with the guilt over the consequences for years. Maybe it had been the damn papers. Receiving them would've been much worse than his ultimatum.

Jesus, she could've gotten them all killed. If Falcon had made a mistake, it could've…

For the thousandth time, his mind ran over the last

mission. Had it gone sideways because of Drew? Or had it all just been shit timing? Didn't mean the guy's head was on straight, though.

He swallowed past his suddenly dry throat and rubbed at the ache in his chest. How could she do that? How could she divorce Drew while he was deployed? She'd always been so loyal. So trustworthy.

God, he'd gotten it all wrong.

What the fuck else had he gotten wrong?

Air refused to fill his lungs as his whole world crashed around him.

Not again. Fuck.

Not again.

Chapter Twenty-One

Unease had settled over Haley's spine after waiting several long minutes out on the porch for Cord. Had she gotten it wrong? Was she supposed to meet him in her office? She finally headed inside, surprised to find him sitting behind her desk, box of condoms on the blotter while he stared at her opened drawer.

"Hey? Where'd you go?" Her smile faded when she saw his ashen face. "What's wrong? Are you okay?"

"No. I'm not." His voice was gravely with raw pain and anger, and it stopped her in her tracks. "I can't believe you were divorcing Drew while we were *deployed*."

She exhaled. Dammit. The divorce papers. She hadn't wanted to taint his friend's memory. "It wasn't like that."

His bark of laughter echoed around them, sounding as hollow as his gaze. "You trying to deny you didn't file for divorce? I can see the damn papers right there."

Oh God. This was a mess. "It wasn't—"

"Yes or no, Haley," he cut her off, tone more angry than hurt now. It was cold and unfeeling and she shivered at the frost entering his gaze.

"Yes, but—"

"No. No buts." He jumped to his feet and scowled at her. "Do you have any idea what that does to a guy who's deployed? Soldiers need support. Need to know everything is good on the homefront so they can fight and carry out their missions without distraction. Not just for themselves, but for their damn teammates and civilians, too." He came around the front of the desk and glared at her. "I trusted you. We *all* trusted you. Shit like this puts the whole team in danger. And now Drew's *dead*."

Air funneled into her tight chest. "You have it all wrong." She took her life in her hands and reached for his arm. "Please, just let me explain."

He yanked out of her grasp and headed for the door. "Forget it."

She followed him into his room and watched helplessly as he threw his belongings haphazardly in his duffle bag. "Drew was cheating on me."

He stiffened but continued to stuff his damn bag. "I know."

Wait…

Her heart lurched. "You knew?"

He stilled and had the good sense to appear ashamed. But then he shrugged it off and zipped up his bag. "Most of the major work is done around here. I think you can manage what's left on the list."

Pain funneled into her chest and she stumbled backward and leaned against the doorframe, nearly doubled over from the intensity. God…she couldn't believe he knew and didn't tell her.

Of *course* his loyalty would've been to Drew and not her.

She shouldn't have trusted him. Shouldn't have done a lot of things with him.

He was no different. In fact, he was worse.

She needed him gone. Needed to breathe.

God, she couldn't breathe.

But she sure as hell wasn't going to let him leave her ranch without hearing her out. She drew herself up to her full height and blocked the doorway. "I filed for divorce six months *before* Drew deployed. He wasn't even living here. And I did not at any time send him papers overseas. He knew they were waiting for him when he returned because he refused to sign the damn things the entire six months before he left."

Cord blinked at her as some of her words started to finally sink in. "You didn't send him anything?"

She fought back a sob at the futility of the situation. "Hell no. I'd never do that. Never put all your lives on the line like that." She sucked in a breath as the pain of his accusation gripped her anew. "God, Cord. I can't believe you'd even think that. I thought you *knew* me."

Seems *she* was the one who was wrong with her trust.

And that hurt. It hurt so bad.

"But the date…" His voice trailed off as he obviously tried to do the math.

"That was the date I asked the lawyer to send me an extra copy, because Drew was so mad he kept shredding them. I wanted a backup for when he returned." She understood how it looked. She really did. But the fact he'd jumped to that conclusion in the first place sat like a fat fist in her throat. And then he hadn't even allowed her a chance to explain, cutting her off, too busy jumping to conclusions. She hadn't even told him everything.

To hell with it. None of it mattered now.

But that wasn't the worst part.

That wasn't the part that hurt so bad tears burned her eyes and throat, and her whole body ached as if she'd been run over by a tank.

He knew. Cord *knew*.

Tears dripped down her face as she turned blindly toward the door. "You can see yourself out."

Without waiting for the rest of it to get through his thick skull, she headed down the hall, slipping into a pair of shorts she grabbed from the basket of clean clothes on her dryer, and stopped by the door long enough to shove her feet into a pair of cowboy boots. Staying inside the house right now wasn't an option. It was killing her. He was killing her.

She wanted to let go. To cry and throw up and cry some more and scream at the world. God, she was tired. So tired. Tired of all the bad shit happening to her. Tired of making wrong choices.

Why had she trusted him with her heart? She'd done it with Drew and he'd stomped all over it. Now Cord had crushed what remained.

She sucked in a deep breath, squared her shoulders, and walked out.

Chapter Twenty-Two

For two days, Cord tried to get back into his old routine of work, work, and more work, with a few shared beers with his buddies. Nothing helped. His mind was messed up good. Christ, he was so confused.

He couldn't remember if he was supposed to be mad at Haley, or if she had the right to be pissed at him.

Probably the latter.

That seemed to be the norm of late.

His inability to trust or give up control had been a source of contention his whole life.

It was after five on Wednesday afternoon and he was in the horse barn, grooming one of the mares. The strokes were soothing to them both. Normally. Not tonight. Not for him.

By the time he finished, he was only mildly aware of a trio of men standing off to the side, watching him with frowns on their faces. Brick wasn't there, but it didn't seem to matter.

Fuck.

He stiffened. He knew what it was—an intervention. Hell, he'd participated in two of them on this ranch this past spring. But they were usually held in Stone's office. There wasn't a chance they'd corner him there. Hell, he hadn't been in the house much except to shower and grab clean clothes. No fucking way could he stand to sleep in his bed. Not with memories of Haley and her soft sighs and heated cries haunting him at every turn.

The barn had a quiet loft big enough for his sleeping bag. He'd slept in worse places. He'd also slept in some amazing ones, too.

More images of Haley and her smiling face washed through his brain.

Behind him, the men kept right on gossiping like women.

"He's not even mumbling to himself."

"Yeah, not good."

"Have the girls had any luck with Haley?"

"Not yet. They're at her place now."

At that, he stiffened and turned to face them. "Leave her alone."

"Ah." A knowing gleam entered Vince's gaze. "So it was *your* fault."

Cord lifted his chin, still too unclear on that point to give an honest answer. "It was a mistake. Leave it at that."

Stone shook his head. "No can do, buddy."

"Why the hell not?" he barked.

"Because we liked you better with Haley," Vince replied. "You were your old self but improved."

"Yeah," Stone said. "It was like having Cord back."

Vince snickered. "The Cord 1.0 version."

He muttered an oath, not at all in the mood for this shit. Straightening, he untied the mare and led her back to her stall then headed to grab the next one. Only, the guys blocked his path.

Squeezing the bridge of his nose, he blew out a breath. "Is there a version of this where you get to the damn point?"

"At least he's still using his words," Vince said cheerfully.

Cord flipped him off.

Stone unfolded his arms and walked closer, grim set to his jaw. "Look, Cord, your sister is worried about you, and frankly, we all are."

Ah hell. He knew that look. His buddy became an immovable wall when he was set on that course. "I'm fine."

"Bullshit," Leo said.

"You might as well spill it." Stone lifted a shoulder. "You know we're not leaving until you do. And you certainly know how big a fuckup my brother and I were in our relationships, so nothing you can tell us will surprise us. We invented the fuckup club. Charter members."

He snorted. Jackasses. But they were good friends, and he remembered the boot being on the other foot. They were only trying to help. Thing was, he wasn't sure if they could. Or if they even should.

Christ, maybe he should take the floor during this Friday's session. They'd probably need at least two hours he was so messed up.

"Everything was great when we left Sunday night," Stone said. "So what happened the next day?"

Jesus, would they ever give it a rest?

No, his mind immediately responded. Thing was, even though he was hurt and angry at Haley, he didn't want the others to regard her with a loss of respect. And then there was the part about Drew and his infidelity. How the hell did he bring that up?

Should he?

Christ, he didn't want to be the one to burst bubbles and ruin memories.

"Damn it, Cord! What the hell did you do?" Stone's angry tone echoed through the barn.

"Drew and Haley were getting a divorce," Cord blurted.

"What?" Vince's raised tone echoed around them.

Leo frowned. "No way."

"Is that what's been eating you?" Stone stepped closer, his gray gaze now dark with turmoil.

"Part of it," Cord finally admitted, since he let the cat half out of the bag

Stone's gray gaze was back on him. "What did Drew do?"

Cord shoved his hands in his hair and blew out a breath. "He fucking cheated on her."

Vince muttered a curse while Leo shook his head sadly.

"I caught him just before that last mission and threatened to tell Haley if he didn't." He scrubbed a hand over his face. "I'm sorry. I was pissed and not thinking straight. I put us all in jeopardy."

"No," Leo said firmly. "It wasn't anything Drew did or didn't do. Trust me. That mission replays in my head all the damn time. It was bad intel. There were more insurgents than reported. Just too damn many."

Cord's chest squeezed tight. He knew in his mind and heart Leo was right, but it would never excuse his foolish behavior.

"Let it go, Warlock," Leo said. "If I've learned anything through our sessions, it's that holding onto the past is unhealthy. Especially something you had no control over."

Vince nodded. "You carried that guilt around long enough. Let it go."

He shook his head. "Not gonna happen. I should've waited until after the mission to confront him."

"Maybe, but it wouldn't have changed the outcome of that day," Stone said, then sighed. "What was Drew thinking? I can't believe he cheated on someone like Haley."

"He did. A lot." Pete's voice drifted down the walkway to them.

They all turned to watch Haley's ranch foreman make his

way to them, still sporting crutches, while Brick walked grimly by his side. So that's where the guy had gone. To Dallas to get Pete.

"Since you were being tight-lipped, I thought we needed to get the scoop from someone who knew what *really* went on at the ranch," Brick said, his gaze not in the least apologetic.

Bastard.

"It's none of our business," he growled, not comfortable about gossiping.

"You're wrong." Brick folded his arms across his chest and dared him to comment. "Haley is our business. *You* are our business, and since the two of you are fucking up a real shot at happiness, you're not leaving us a whole lot of choice."

"I'm not a fan of nattering, but there are things I think you need to know," Pete said, his gaze serious and mouth grim. "Ever since Haley inherited the ranch, her life has changed. She found a purpose. Found her home. She didn't want to travel and wander anymore. That's why she gave up her job with that blog."

"And Drew wasn't happy," Leo said.

Pete shook his head. "No, he wasn't. He tried to make her sell the place, but she refused, insisting he was gone half the time, anyway. She tried to make their marriage work. She dropped everything when he was home. But Drew was going through the money like water, spending it on one trip after another, until she was in financial trouble."

Anger rose swift in Cord. That must've been when she'd had to sell her horse. And then the rest of the horses.

"Finally, she put her foot down again and stopped going. He didn't." The older man sighed and shook his head. "Then the cheating started. So she filed for divorce, but he wouldn't sign. Kept putting it off, shredding the documents, coming up with excuse after excuse, angry that she didn't understand. He didn't want a divorce. He wanted her back, but I think the damage was too severe."

Trust was broken. Once that happened, it was hard to get it back. Hard as hell to take a chance again…

Pete drew in a breath and shook his head. "I wish I didn't have to say more, but I love Haley like my own daughter, just as her uncle had, and I don't want you thinking badly of her." The man turned his attention on him. "And if she's fallen for you, Cord, you need to know the whole truth so you can fix whatever you've done."

He nodded as his twisted insides tightened further.

"What's the rest?" Stone asked.

"After he died, and the death benefit was paid out, she only received half." Pete's voice trailed off after dropping that bombshell.

"Who got the other half?" he asked, already knowing he wasn't going to like the answer. Drew's parents were dead and he'd had no siblings.

Pete's gaze snapped to him. "His son."

Fuck. He tried to draw in a breath, but it was no use. Not with the fist-sized lump lodged in his throat.

"What?"

"He had a son?"

"With who?"

Pete nodded to the men all speaking at once again. "Some girl he met on one of those adventures, I guess."

Son-of-a-bitch. Cord leaned back against the stall as the world tilted. Now he got it. Now he understood Drew's last words. Yes, Haley sure as hell had deserved a hell of a lot better. And dammit, he'd gone and hurt the woman, too.

Cord closed his eyes, reeling as all of it fell into place, and he stood out as a number one jackass. Somehow, after all the pain Drew had caused, she'd managed to find it in her to trust him, not only with her body, but with her heart. He'd seen it in her eyes. Felt it in her touch, and he'd blown it by walking out on her—just like Drew.

Damn. He opened his eyes and muttered a curse. What had he done?

"How could he have been such an idiot?" Vince frowned, anger darkening the Italian's face. A rarity, and something one did not want to mess with if they were smart.

"God only knows," Pete said. He turned to Cord. "So, now that you know everything, what's your plan to win her back?"

Turn back time. Because he wasn't sure he could fix things without removing his words, his stupid distrust from the other day.

"Hey," Brick said. "Stone and I both thought we'd fucked up too bad to fix things, but we managed. I'm sure you can, too."

Stone shook his head. "Unfortunately, Haley's a lot like him. Stubborn."

Yeah, he knew. He ran a hand through his hair again, trying to figure out a solution.

How do you fix trust?

"Apologize," Leo said. "It might not fix everything, but it'll get the conversation started and give you an opening to make her see you're sorry."

"And tell her you love her," Brick added. "You do, don't you?"

"Yes," he admitted without hesitation. "I have for years."

Vince rolled his eyes. "'Bout fucking time you realized that, Warlock."

He snorted. "Yeah. But it's too late."

"No, never too late," Stone insisted. "So what, exactly, happened?"

With a sigh, Cord gave in and recanted his idiocy.

Brick grimaced. "I hate to admit it, but I would've jumped to that conclusion, too."

"Me, too," Stone said. "We were Rangers for years, Cord.

You don't just turn that off. Of course our minds would automatically think of our team. That's how we survived. That said…damn, man, you were an idiot."

He choked out a laugh at the understatement of the decade. He was an idiot. An idiot who was in love with a sweet woman who deserved better. Who deserved someone who loved her unconditionally. Someone who gave without wanting in return. Someone who would fulfill her every need, dream, fantasy, desire.

For a while there, he had been those things to her. Now, he had to find a way to do it again. To give her everything. To make up for fucking walking out on her.

He stilled as several thoughts occurred.

Everything. That's what he was going to give her.

He pushed from the wall and turned to face Pete. "I need your help."

Chapter Twenty-Three

The day of the grand opening of Haley's Haven arrived with the sun shining brightly in a cloudless sky. The vendors were all set up and ready to go under tents that lined her front yard. Vince was even there with free cannoli, but none of it held the same appeal as it had last week.

As much as she hated to admit it, Haley felt…broken. Shattered. Like she'd never be whole again. Drew's infidelity had devastated her, but it never ripped her apart. Not like Cord's… God, she didn't even know what to call what he'd done.

His mistrust? And the fact he'd—

No. She wasn't going there again. Wasn't going to linger in that hell that had no answers.

But she knew why it had hurt. She knew why it was hell. She'd fallen in love with the man. And it sucked that she'd realized too late.

Somehow, she was going to put on her game face and make it a good day. Eventually she'd get her smile back. Her love for the ranch. It would all resurface. It had to, otherwise…

Nope. She wasn't going there, either. No more *otherwises*. And before she could change her mind, she walked over to Beth and Jovy, who were enjoying Vince's dessert without her. Time to change that, too.

"Ah, there's the woman of the hour." Vince grinned, holding out a cannoli. "I can't believe you've passed them up three times already. There's nothing wrong with them, is there?" He turned the plate around to examine his creation.

She grabbed the plate and gave him one of her smiles. Although her favorite dessert in the world currently tasted like cardboard, she moaned and gave it a thumbs-up.

Everything she'd eaten that week tasted like cardboard, so she figured she wasn't really lying to him with her approval.

"Well, it looks like your day is already a success," Jovy observed, nodding toward the crowd and the line of horses Brick, Stone, and Leo, along with a few of the veteran candidates they had in mind for permanent work, were sweet enough to volunteer to register. The guys wanted to take care of that part of the business today so they could watch the candidates in action.

Since she had all the enthusiasm of a rock, she'd agreed.

It was times like these she really missed Gypsy. All week, Haley had needed her horse's company. Galloping across the field at breakneck speeds, wind in her hair, sun beating down. Her chest tightened at that loss. Someday, she would own a horse again.

"I saw the plans for your cabins," Vince said, breaking into her thoughts. "I think they're a great idea. And the fact you hired vets to build them is a wonderful thing, too."

She smiled, this one more genuine, since she was happy to finally put Drew's money to good use. Not that she'd needed his approval, but knowing the money representing his loss of life—which was how her two smart friends, Beth and Jovy, had told her to look at it—was used to help other veterans, somehow made the endeavor sweeter.

"Haley, girl," Pete said, from behind her.

"Pete!" She gasped and turned to hug her dear friend, careful not to knock him down. "How are you?"

"Going stir crazy," he grumbled. "Still have at least two more damn months to go before they'll even consider taking this cast off."

She reached out to set a hand on his arm. "Well, just do what they say. I want you better and back here where you belong."

"You sure you're going to need me?"

She reeled back. "Of course I will. I'll always need you. You're family."

His eyes grew a little misty at that.

"So, what do you think about the turnout?" she asked, changing the subject for him. She knew he didn't like to get too mushy.

Kind of like another hardheaded man she knew.

Her hollow insides compressed, and it felt like her chest was about to cave in on itself. She inhaled deep to fill the empty space with air. Despite the fact he'd hurt her, she'd missed the jerk so damn much. God, she was an idiot for it, too. But she did miss him.

Since Monday evening, she'd replayed that whole fiasco over and over, and she had to admit, some of it was her fault. If she had been upfront with the guys when they'd first retired and dropped by to fix up the ranch, then perhaps some of this could've been avoided.

Still didn't change the fact he never told you about Drew cheating, her mind insisted, as it had all week.

But she wasn't his concern. Drew was.

And that was also true.

So, round and round, those thoughts chased each other until she was too exhausted to think.

Unfortunately, she could still feel.

"Looks like you have yet another customer." Vince's gaze twinkled as he nodded behind her.

This would make lucky number thirteen if she had her count correct. Turning around to watch the check-in process, she sucked in a breath as all the air on earth vanished the instant Cord climbed out of his truck.

Oh God. Why was he here? And with a horse trailer, no less.

He couldn't possibly think boarding his horse here was a good idea. At-Ease was a great place for it. Besides, she didn't want his horse here. Correction. She didn't want *him* here.

Her mind raced to figure out a way to refuse him service, but she knew she couldn't do it in front of all his friends. Or even strangers.

Why was he putting her in this position?

The urge to flee was so strong her body vibrated. As if reading her mind or body language or whatever the hell Warlock used, he stepped in front of her, using his big, sexy body to block her escape.

"Haley." His voice was low and his gaze remorseful, and dammit, it still managed to send goose bumps over her skin.

She wanted to ask him what he was doing there. No. She wanted to ask him to leave. But her stupid throat was tight and burning because just looking at him made her ache.

"I'm so damn sorry," he said, the rigid line of his shoulders matching the tightness around his mouth and eyes.

Her heart cracked open for him, and that pissed her off. All week it had been shriveled up tight…because of him.

She couldn't do it. She couldn't stand there and pretend to have a conversation with him. Dragging in a lungful of air, she stepped backward, planning to escape around the crowd, but she hit a brick wall. Spinning, she noted that was exactly who she'd hit. Brick. Vince was there with Pete, too. Surrounding her. Jovy, Beth, and Stone rounded out the traitors rallying around Cord.

Okay, she could forgive Beth—he was her brother. But the rest? Damn them. She was outnumbered. Outmaneuvered, and God, she was tired. So freaking tired.

"I'm a Ranger, Haley," Cord continued. "Doesn't matter that I'm no longer active duty. With training ingrained in me to have my team member's backs, it never goes away. That's why my mind immediately shot to them when I first saw the date on your divorce papers."

Okay. The date thing was a problem. She understood his concern. She turned back to him. "It's the fact you thought I'd do that to all of you that hurts. It hurts bad."

Her voice wobbled. Dammit.

He clenched his jaw and his fists, and she got the impression he wanted to hold her.

Oh hell no. She couldn't take that.

"I'm sorry about that, too. I realized how wrong I was once my head cleared, along with my stupidity."

"Sometimes that takes a while," Beth interjected. "Brick gets that way, too."

"And Stone," Jovy added, much to their men's grumbles.

Haley knew it was an alpha male thing. But five whole days had gone by without so much as a call or text or…token cannoli. All of those would've gone a long way to breaking her down. Instead, she got what he was good at. Silence.

Well, she deserved more than that. She deserved—

"My heart," he said, as if reading her mind. "I buried it. Packed it away with no intention of ever letting it see the light of day. I had my family to worry about. That was enough. And then you come along with your sweet, genuine smile and shook it loose. You've always ruled my heart with that smile of yours, Haley. I used to think Drew was the luckiest bastard in the world, and I hadn't realized how right I was until *I* was the luckiest bastard."

Oh damn. That was good. She sniffed. "Go on."

A small twinge tugged the corner of his mouth. "And then I hurt you, too. And I'm so damn sorry, Haley. If I could go back and do it over I would, although I'm an ass and would probably mess it up twice. So I'd prefer to own up to my mistake and beg your forgiveness with the promise I'll make it up to you for the rest of your life."

Well hell.

She blinked. And sniffed. That was good, too. "Who are you and what have you done with Cord?"

His mouth twitched into a smile. "You happened, Haley. You and your unselfish caring and giving ways. It made me want to be better. Made me want to be all the things I saw in your eyes. And yet I failed you."

She drew in a breath and decided to lay it out there. Tell him why it was so hard to let go of her hurt. "Do you know where you failed?"

"Everywhere."

"No. It's the fact you knew." She shook her head and swiped at the tears that escaped down her cheeks. "You had Drew's back. I understand he was your teammate, but I thought I was your friend, too. It was the fact you knew about his infidelity, Cord. You knew and never told me."

He shook his head and stepped close. "I didn't tell you because I had no idea you knew, or that you were getting a divorce. I didn't want to tarnish his memory for you."

"Isn't that why you never told them about the divorce, or cheating, or his son, Haley?" Pete asked quietly.

She sucked in a breath, and because it felt like the ground was opening up underneath her, she reached out and grasped the nearest thing. Vince. She gripped his arm tight as she confronted Pete. "You told them about his son?"

"Yes," Pete replied, and his betrayal caught her by

surprise. She knew he'd done it out of love, but right now, she was too raw to process it. "They know everything, and you've gotten some things wrong. Please hear him out."

Cord took a deep breath and looked her dead in the eye. "The day I found out about Drew's cheating was the day of our last mission."

Her heart rocked. He hadn't known for months?

"I threatened him," he admitted, guilt deepening his tone.

That somehow made her feel better…and worse. Guilt was such a heavy thing to carry. She knew it firsthand.

"What kind of threat?" she asked, finding it hard to comprehend, and yet, she could see the honesty and conviction in his eyes.

"I told him when the mission was over he was calling you to confess, and if he didn't, I would. But he never got the chance, and since you already knew, it probably wouldn't have meant anything."

That was where he was wrong. And now she was beginning to see she'd had it all wrong, too. God. He'd had her back. "You were going to make him call me?"

He nodded, anger from that memory still lingered in his eyes. "I was so pissed at him. He was the luckiest man I knew and he was throwing it all away. He had you. He had everything."

"Damn." She inhaled and the tears dripped once again. "That was really, really good." She released Vince and took a step toward Cord. "You only found out that day?"

"Yes."

She stepped closer. "You think I'm everything?"

"Haley." He reached out to cup her face, and his eyes softened. The sheer force of emotion in his gaze made her knees wobble. "I *know* you're everything."

The last of her pain disappeared under the honesty in his eyes and those beautiful words that bared his heart and soul.

In front of everyone.

Her Warlock didn't hold back. He laid it all out there. Fought for her. Made her see she'd had it wrong.

"I'm sorry," she said. "So sorry. I thought you knew for years."

"No. Hell no. I've *loved* you for years."

She sucked in a breath and tried to see his eyes, but her damn waterworks broke again. "You love me?"

Still holding her face, he gently kissed them away. "I do," he said, then brushed her mouth, her tears making his lips taste salty. "Very much."

"I love you, too."

A growl emanated in his throat a second before his kiss turned intense, deep, hot enough to send shouts and cheers around the crowd. And if her lips hadn't been otherwise preoccupied, she would've joined in.

When they finally broke for air, he set his forehead to hers and kissed her nose. "I have a surprise for you."

She drew back to smile at him. "You already gave me everything I could ever possibly want or need."

Confusion wrinkled his brow. "What?"

"Your trust," she replied simply. "That's the best thing you could ever give me. I don't want anything else."

A wicked gleam entered his eyes. "You sure about that?"

Heat spread out, warming the deep freeze from her body. "Okay, let me rephrase that. I don't *need* anything else. But there is a lot of you I want, and I'll take that every day and twice on Tuesday."

"Only twice?" He smiled. "You're slipping."

She smacked his shoulder. "Didn't you say something about a surprise for me?"

"Yes." He grabbed her hand and tugged her through the crowed to his truck, then stopped in the front. "Stay here."

She nodded, and he went around to the back of the horse

trailer.

Her heart dropped to her stomach then raced in her suddenly too tight chest. "You got me a horse?"

No one had ever done anything like that for her before.

"Not just any horse," he said, walking toward her, leading the most beautiful horse in the world.

She gasped. "Gypsy?" Stepping close, Haley hardly dared to blink in case all of this incredible morning had been just a dream. But it *was* her horse, the one she'd been forced to sell nearly three years ago. The tears were flowing now as Gypsy caught her scent and nudged her with her nose. "How?"

"Pete helped me track her down," Cord replied, setting a big hand on the small of her back. His touch reassuring and warm and strong.

"I don't understand how this day went from awful to amazing, but God, I'm so grateful. So damn grateful."

Cord turned her around and brushed a finger across her cheek to tuck a loose strand of hair behind her ear. "I want you to know that I meant what I said before. You really are everything to me."

"Even though I'm stubborn and jump to wrong conclusions?"

"*Especially* because you're stubborn and jump to wrong conclusions."

The empty, hollow space in her chest was now full to bursting. "Another good answer." She gently tugged his face closer and kissed the man of her dreams, next to the horse of her dreams, on the ranch of her dreams, and Haley knew she didn't need to dream anymore, because she had the real deal. She had everything.

She had the right Ranger.

Epilogue

A month with the right woman made all the difference in the world to Cord's life and his outlook on that life. Loving and being loved by Haley was a gift, one he'd never take for granted. She brought a smile to his face and a contentedness to his heart that went a long way to quieting that darkness that used to so often invade. Acknowledging some hard truths about his dead friend had been important, too.

He knew Drew had loved Haley in his own way. He'd just loved her wrong. Not a mistake Cord would ever make. He'd waited too long to get his chance, and now that he had the beautiful, giving woman in his life, he was not going to mess it up again. Once was bad enough, but he'd learned his lesson and he was a quick learner. Honesty and communication were key and rules he lived by now.

"I can't believe we're getting married soon," Jovy said, wrapping her arms around Stone who pulled her in for a kiss.

"What about you two?" Brick asked. "Are you tying the knot this year, too?"

Ever since Brick popped the question the previous

week—and his sister had said yes—the two kept throwing hints to him and Haley to take the plunge.

"Yeah, you're already living together, why not make it legal?" Stone grinned.

After Haley's Haven opened and Haley forgave him for being an idiot, Cord hadn't spent a night anywhere else. At-Ease was special to him and he was damn proud of what they were accomplishing, but it no longer required his presence twenty-four-seven. He decided to commute from Haley's and hadn't regretted it once.

Besides, she came first in his life now, and he was the luckiest son-of-a-bitch, because she always put him first, too.

A simple rule that made all the difference in the world.

"So, is that a yes? A maybe? Perhaps?" his sister prodded, slipping her arm around Brick and leaning into him as they all relaxed in the rec room after that week's session.

Jovy nodded. "Beth just wants to see you happy."

"I *am* happy." Evidence of it warmed his chest and surely it reached his eyes, because he no longer held anything back.

"I can see that." His sister's gaze grew misty and she sniffed.

Brick stiffened and panic crossed his face. "Ah hell, Cord. Did you have to make your sister cry? You know I don't do tears."

He laughed. "Good luck. My sister feels things deeply. She's always going to have a tear in her eye." He winked at her. "She also has deep feelings about spiders, so you'd better prepare your eardrums."

Lizzie punched his arm. "Brick is well aware how deeply I feel things, and trust me, he isn't complaining."

Cord groaned. She had to play the tease-my-brother-about-sex-with-his-buddy card.

"Okay." Haley joined them, running her hand up his back. "How about we talk about the wedding. When is your friend arriving from Philadelphia?"

"Tomorrow." Jovy grinned. "She's bringing my cat, finally. An hers, too, since they've become buddies."

Vince stiffened. "Cat? Uh…and it'll be staying here?"

"Yeah." Jovy frowned. "They both will, until…Oh no, don't tell me you're allergic."

"Okay, I won't. But I am." Vince grimaced. "Sorry."

Cord smiled. "Since your friend is staying in my old room, maybe she can keep the cats in there for a while until you figure out a solution."

Vince pointed at him. "What he said. Listen to Warlock. He's wise."

Both Brick and Stone groaned.

"Okay, now that that's solved," Beth said. "What role is Lula Belle playing?"

"I was thinking about making her my best man," Stone teased, and received a backhand across the chest from his fiancée. "What? I said best man, not my best girl. You'll always be my best girl, Jovy."

For that he received a totally different kind of smack. Right on the lips.

Haley shifted into Cord, and when he leaned in to kiss her temple he felt her chuckle. He drew back to catch her gaze, but it was trained outside the French doors, where the cow in question was rearranging Jovy's flowers. Again.

It'd become a ritual with those two over the past few weeks. Sooner or later, something was going to give…most likely someone's patience.

"Hey, Jovy, here's an idea," Haley said, winking up at him before returning her attention to the soon-to-be bride and nodding at the door. "What if Lula Belle was your flower girl?"

A curse left Jovy's lips when she saw the mess the cow was making of her garden. "That's it." She released Stone and moved so fast even Cord had trouble tracking the spitfire. She reached under the couch, pulled out a water gun bigger than her arm, then marched for the door Beth opened just in time for the determined woman.

"Okay, Lula Belle. Game on."

Acknowledgments

A huge thank you to my editor, Heather Howland, for all your time, patience, and suggestions for helping me make Cord and Haley the very best they could be! I love them together!

Once again, I'd like to thank the whole Lovestruck team! Working with everyone at Entangled makes writing fun. You all rock!

To my husband, family, and cats for supporting my "writing" habit/addiction. Love you all!

A big shout out to the Minions, and the Hoods! You know who you are!

And, finally, to you, the readers, thank you for your support, the kind words, and wonderful reviews. This one's for you.

About the Author

Donna Michaels is an award winning, *New York Times* & *USA Today* bestselling author of *Romaginative* fiction. Her hot, humorous, and heartwarming stories include cowboys, men in uniform, and some sexy, primal alphas. With a husband in the military fulltime, and a household of nine, she never runs out of material to write and has rightfully earned the nickname Lucy…and sometimes Ethel. From short to epic, her books entertain readers across a variety of sub-genres, and one was even hand drawn into a Japanese translation. Now, if only she could read it.

To learn more about Donna Michaels and her books, or to join her mailing list, visit www.DonnaMichealsAuthor.com.

Thanks for reading,
~Donna

Discover* The Men of At Ease Ranch *series…

In a Ranger's Arms

Her Secret Ranger

Find love in unexpected places with these satisfying Lovestruck reads…

THE WRONG KIND OF COMPATIBLE
a *Lover Undercover* novel by Kadie Scott

For undercover FBI agent Drew Kerrigan, computers have always made more sense than people, but he'd better develop some slick social skills in a hurry if he's going to win over the brilliant, too-tantalizing-for-his-sanity data analyst Cassie Howard. Hacking their systems was easy. Now he's just got to hack the one person in the company most likely to see through his ruse…

BETTING THE BAD BOY
a *Behind the Bar* novel by Stefanie London

Paige Thomas needs to find a job—*any* job—to make ends meet. Noah Reid is looking after his best friend's bar for one month, and he can't do it alone. Things get steamy when Noah hires Paige, but she bets him that she can keep her hands to herself while they work together. Too bad for her, Noah is an expert at breaking the rules…

BLAME IT ON THE KISS
a *Kisses in the Sand* novel by Robin Bielman

When Honor Mitchell promises to do the things on her dying best friend's wish list, she's determined to follow through. Then she's thrown together for wedding duties with the one man who complicates her vow—just by looking at him. Bryce Bishop's trust in women is shot, but he can't help but help Honor tick off the items on his ex's list, even if it puts him in a no-win situation. He'll help Honor get what she wants...even if being the do-good guy puts his plans—and heart—in jeopardy.

DRUNK ON YOU
a *Bourbon Boys* novel by Teri Anne Stanley

Justin Morgan would happily drown the pain of his injured leg—and the guilt he brought back from Afghanistan—in bourbon. Except, there won't *be* any booze if he doesn't rescue his family's century-old distillery from financial ruin. The problem? Allie McGrath, the youngest daughter of the distillery's co-owners and the one woman he can't have. If he can't keep their attraction under control, there's a solid chance they'll send the whole enterprise crumbling to the ground...if he doesn't crash and burn first.

94836946R00121

Made in the USA
Columbia, SC
03 May 2018